"I told you I wouldn't be one of your trophies!"

Hurt and furiously angry, Lacey bit out the words.

Luke snapped harshly, "You, one of *my* trophies! That's a laugh. The way you behaved tonight, I'm beginning to think you're one of the groupies who have a hit list of celebrities to work through." At her outraged gasp, he dragged her closer. "But you're something new, Lacey. Most of them usually follow through when they've put the goods on the line."

She slapped him then, an unsatisfactory blow impeded by her lack of elbow room, but one that made his eyes blaze.

"You left it a little late to change your mind," he said, pushing her backward so she fell on the bed. "In fact, *too* late."

Winter Sun, Summer Rain

Ann Charlton

Harlequin Books

TORONTO • NEW YORK • LONDON
AMSTERDAM • PARIS • SYDNEY • HAMBURG
STOCKHOLM • ATHENS • TOKYO • MILAN

Original hardcover edition published in 1984
by Mills & Boon Limited

ISBN 0-373-02701-X

Harlequin Romance first edition July 1985

CHAPTER ONE

WHEN she was fourteen, Lacey threw her arms out and told her best friend Marie the secret she'd carried around for months. 'I love Luke Harrow,' she cried and turned bright red as soon as she revealed herself.

The press clippings of him, frozen in action at Wimbledon or smilingly holding aloft a trophy at White City were glued into her Luke Harrow scrapbook. Behind her clothes on her wardrobe wall was pinned a giant poster, paid for by thrifty re-allotments of her allowance. Every time she changed—which was often— Lacey would sweep aside her dresses and uniforms as if they were stage curtains, to gaze upon the colour pin-up of her own private Greek god. Fair, waving hair and bronze skin. Tall and athletic, with a profile to make a teenager cry. Not that Lacey did that. She was far more likely to emerge from her bedroom and sit at the breakfast table wreathed in dreamy aloofness while her father chided her for playing her radio too loud again.

Even when Luke's fans turned their backs on him, Lacey didn't forget him. In fact when she read the sad half column about Luke Harrow after all the fuss and scandal about the accident in which his father was killed, she sent him a photograph of herself. Marie took it for her under oath of silence and it was developed along with her school sports day snaps. Lacey posed against the old quince tree with a poster in her hands. '*I love you Luke*' was printed on it. It was a bold move but one that would, she hoped, show him that not everyone was ready to believe the worst of him. Of course she never got a reply which disappointed her at first. But she turned fifteen, sixteen then seventeen and Luke Harrow proved to be just the first of her teenage crushes. The poster behind her clothes stayed but others went up on the walls. She went through a nostalgia kick and hung up Bogart and Bergman in a Casablanca poster, collected pictures of the timeless Stones and Sean Connery and countless pop groups that burst into the top forty and sank as quickly into obscurity.

At nineteen she packed her bags to leave home for her own flat. She threw out the Stones and the others but kept Luke's picture and scrapbook with the memorabilia stored in her mother's spare room. He had made her different—she had been the only girl in her group whose favourite man was a tennis player that year—that crucial fourteenth year when others were drawn to the sulky attractions of pop stars and actors.

'Oh—Luke Harrow—sure he's good looking but he's too, you know, *nice*' her friends said. And the ultimate condemnation, 'Even my *parents* like Saint Luke.' Lacey liked it that way. She *wanted* to be the only one and the distinction was almost as good as watching him play on television. So his photographs had not joined the others in the fire.

She turned twenty, twenty-one and the years quickened to twenty-five. The men in her life were no longer pin-ups on a wall to be gazed at between school uniforms and jeans. They were real, flesh and blood and a whole lot more trouble and fun than a mere photograph. But Luke Harrow had been the first man in her life. The one who woke her from childhood dreaming to an awareness of boys and love and life— and herself. . . .

'Well? Can you do it or can't you?' her prospective client rapped out and Lacey jumped to attention. She had missed half of what he'd said.

'Before the end of summer?' She leafed through the builder's plans and drawings that he had pushed at her.

'By Christmas preferably. You don't seem to be listening, Miss Teale.'

'I'm sorry if I appear vague. I do have two other assignments for that time and I'm trying to think how I could fit in another by Christmas . . . perhaps if you could give me some idea of the extent of your . . .?'

She stopped as his secretary buzzed him and he barked a few words in to the intercom.

'Miss Teale.' He got up and walked to the door,

making it clear that this initial interview was over. She straightened the drawings and rose from the visitor's chair. 'I don't want to be *fitted* in with anyone else. If you can't see your way clear to occupy a guest room at Fremont for the time it takes to supervise the work I want, then I shall have to consider another decorator. Which would be a pity. I like your style. However, I suggest you consider re-shuffling your other commitments. It might be worth your time.'

The sarcastic edge to his voice surprised her. But with his money he could afford a little sarcasm. Lacey smoothed down the fabric of her skirt. Another difficult client in the making she thought and wished she could say no right now and save herself a lot of trouble. Of course she couldn't do that. Mike wouldn't let her refuse this job even if they did it for chickenfeed. Her partner was alive to the importance of decorating the homes of the rich and famous. That way the name of Logan and Teale Interiors was bandied about where it did the most good.

'Naturally, Mr——' she began.

He looked at his watch. 'Something urgent has come up, Miss Teale. Phone me will you?' He hardly even glanced at her and Lacey swallowed her annoyance. A client was a client.

'Certainly. Logan and Teale will be happy to decorate your home at the time you specify. I'll phone you tomorrow to arrange our preliminary meeting regarding your preferences on——'

'Yes, yes, Miss Teale. That sounds fine. Good morning.'

She turned slightly as she passed him in the doorway and he looked at her though she didn't think he was seeing beyond the lenses of her glasses.

'Good morning—Mr Harrow.'

So much for youthful idols, she thought on her way back to the offices of Logan and Teale. The fair, waving hair was maybe a fraction darker but thick and cared for—his skin was bronze as of course it would be for he did not spend all his time nursing his commercial ventures along. He was still basically an outdoors man, coaching at his tennis ranch, though he had not played publicly since the accident and the press' indictment of him. But the golden personality of Luke Harrow was gone. The easy smile and humourous banter that had made him almost as famous as his sporting skill, had vanished. It was sad that he had soured Lacey thought, remembering his wit and the generous reception he had always given the press even at their most intrusive.

Of course he had reason to be bitter. The press had put him on a pedestal, revelled in his blue-eyed good looks, sportsmanship and the lack of temperament that belied the on-court killer instinct. The same press had pulled him down in double quick time and stomped on him. But it was ten years ago. Luke Harrow's mouth was still harsh with it, his manner abrasive, rude. Unnecessarily rude. Face it Lacey—your girlhood hero is an objectionable, overbearing brute who was going to make a very difficult customer. Somehow she would have to work closely with this new Luke Harrow and put aside any old memories of that golden young man framed between her size eight sports slip and disco dress.

'How was your pin-up?' Mike asked, looking around from a pile of carpet samples.

Lacey tossed her bag down and perched on the edge of his desk. 'I'm sorry I told you about that,' she sighed, 'You won't let me forget it, will you?' She had admitted to being a fan but hadn't told him that she'd actually proclaimed her love to Wimbledon's darling in a photograph. Even now, at twenty-five, that seemed a private thing. Ridiculous, but private to the girl she had been at fourteen—another person light years away.

'Oh—oh,' Mike searched her face. 'Not so good?'

Lacey took a deep breath. 'Let's put it this way, Mike. If Luke Harrow wasn't indecently wealthy—if he hadn't bought the most fantastic old house that I've fantasised over since I was a kid—and if we could do without the money *and* the prestige of the job. . . .'

'Yes?'

'I'd tell him to go clout himself with a jumbo racquet—or——'

'Uh—huh. I get the picture. What you need is coffee.' Mike went to pour some from the ever ready percolator. He came back with it and held out a cup to Lacey who paced back and forth.

'What a pig he is, Mike! I can't believe it.' She passed his outstretched hand and didn't pause. Mike looked down at the coffee and thoughtfully back to Lacey's tense figure.

'Do you know,' she rounded on him suddenly and took off her glasses, 'I don't believe he looked at me—I mean *really* looked at me once? How on earth am I going to decorate his house for him if he doesn't even recognise me as human? "Miss Teale",' she assumed a deep voice and mocked Luke Harrow's impatient tones, ' "I don't want to be *fitted* in with anyone else." He actually wants me to go and live in at the house to supervise the job—can you imagine?' She paced away again, thrusting the glasses back on to her nose so that they perched halfway down. 'Fancy living in the same house with *that* bad-tempered devil. . . .'

'He seems to have got under your skin, Lacey, darling.' Mike put the coffee into her hand. 'I don't recall you ever getting so uptight.'

'No. Well——' She sipped her coffee and looked at him over the glasses. 'It isn't often that I find myself snapped at as if I was a private in one man's army. And I just sat there and let him! I have the feeling that Mr Harrow is not going to be an easy man to please.' She saw the look on Mike's face and held up one hand. 'Okay, okay, I know. He's a customer and an important one and we *will* please him if we have to stand on our heads. In spite of great provocation I was very amenable. Yes, Mr Harrow—of *course*, Mr Harrow, three bags full, Mr Harrow——'

Mike laughed.

'I'm glad you find it funny, partner,' she snapped.

'If you'd given him a burst of those green eyes he would have really looked at you. Why do you insist on wearing your glasses all the time? You only need them for close work.'

'I don't wear them *all* the time. Just for business.

Clients like the image. Why I don't know, but spectacles and a smoothed back hairdo inculcate confidence.'

Mike ran a hand over his own helmet of tightly curled brown hair—a throwback to a Greek grandmother. '*Now* she tells me.' His lugubrious expression brought a low laugh from her.

'You know very well what I mean. And you, Mike Logan, you heartbreaker, manage all those matrons with impeccable style, glasses or no glasses.'

He made a mock bow. 'Thank you, ma'am. Seriously though, you can't hide behind those blinkers forever, Lacey.'

'Hide?'

'That's what I said.' He went back to his carpet samples, tossing one or two over critically before looking back at her, 'You really are a paradox. Poised and confident on the one hand—shy on the other.'

'Oh come on, Mike. Don't be silly. I'm not at all shy.'

'Mmm, I think you are. With men.'

'Ha. I'm not at all shy about saying no.'

'I know,' he nodded with emphasis. 'That's just the point, darling. I think maybe you're too shy about saying yes.'

She held his eyes for a moment and turned away, wishing this hadn't come up again. 'We agreed, Mike, from the start—that this was to be a business arrangement and it has worked very well. . . .'

He shrugged. 'No harm in reviewing business arrangements from time to time . . . we could easily extend our partnership. Some nights I get lonely in my little flat upstairs,' he added plaintively at her withdrawn expression. Lacey smiled, grateful for his tacked-on humour. Mike really was very nice—special—but just not special enough.

'Little flat,' she snorted. 'You could film the charge of the Light Brigade in your bedroom.'

'That's not what I had in mind,' he grinned. 'And how come a nice girl like you is speaking so familiarly about my bedroom anyway? People might talk.'

Lacey waved a careless hand, glad to be back on their

old footing. 'Oh, darling, I can tell you intimate details about a hundred bedrooms. After all I specialise in them.'

'Yes. Ironic, isn't it?'

She picked up her bag and walked through to her own work area and her cheeks were flushed. Mike was probably right. She could be clinging to outmoded standards. But though she was fond of him, very fond, it wasn't enough to make her want to share his bed, even though some of her friends might take lovers with as little hesitation as they would over buying a weekly magazine. Perhaps she would stay forever a career-woman, hiding behind Dior glasses, decorating bedrooms for other people's affairs . . . and wondering why the men in her life had never really made her blood race or her control slip.

'I can understand why he changed. But why so radically?' she mused seconds later and as she took out her notes made that morning, she quite missed Mike's arrested gaze and her own erratic train of thought.

'Harrow,' the voice snapped when she was put through to their newest client the following day. Harrow. How appropriate. The whole business could be just that. Harrowing. She would have to use her best technique to achieve any workable client–decorator relationship with him.

'Good morning, Mr Harrow,' she said in her sweetest tones. 'This is Lacey Teale. I'm phoning to arrange a suita——'

'Who?'

Lacey swallowed, gripped the phone a little harder and took off her glasses. Her very *best* technique, she reminded herself. Mike, with a prospective client, paused to eye her.

'Lacey Teale, Mr Harrow. Of Logan and Teale Interiors——' The hand holding her glasses tapped rapidly and she forced a smile to her mouth. Mike grinned and gave her the thumbs up sign and received an unladylike grimace as he saw one of his matrons to the door. When he came back Lacey had replaced the receiver and her hand was still over it, knuckles pale.

'Well, I shall be meeting our newest client tonight for a preliminary chat,' she said tightly. 'Or maybe I mean—preliminary snap.'

'Tonight?'

'Yes. Mr Harrow is unable to fit me into his busy schedule for a week otherwise.' Lacey stared at her partner. 'Mike—I wouldn't normally admit this, but I don't know if I can handle this one.'

'Why—do you think you might be tempted to say yes to your one-time heart throb?' he said flippantly and dropped into the visitor's chair in front of her desk.

'Mike!' Her colour rose and she flicked an angry glance at him as she opened the slim Harrow file. 'I mean the job as you very well know. How can I come up with sympathetic layouts and designs for a man who communicates on a sergeant-major level? Unless I can form some sort of understanding with him it'll be virtually useless trying to do anything as personal as decorate his home. And I'm darned if I'll do a hack job just for the money.'

'We can't let him go elsewhere, Lacey, and it's no good handing it over to me. That style of house is your specialty.'

'Well just don't be too surprised if I call for help will you?'

Mike looked at her rather closely then levered his long, thin body from the steel-framed chair. 'If Harrow looks anywhere as good as he used to, I rather hope you *will* call for help.' Lacey's eyebrows shot up in surprise at the dry, ambiguous comment but Mike just grinned again and went to answer his phone.

The meeting place was a restaurant. Rather small, rather full for mid-week, and more than rather expensive. Lacey didn't need to see the menu to mentally kiss goodbye to a huge chunk of her monthly expenses budget. It stood to reason that Logan and Teale would be paying and she hoped that Luke Harrow intended to spend freely on his house and prove worth it. 'Join me for dinner,' he'd barked on the phone and when she'd hesitated over the prospect of a couple of hours of indigestion, added impatiently, 'I have to eat and I suppose you do too. We might as well use that time.'

He sounded in some doubt as to whether she needed to eat. As if she might be some sort of miracle robot that smiled in response to snappish ex-champions and could produce designs at will regardless of a full workload. He certainly hadn't looked at her as if she was alive. 'Actually, I run on oil,' she'd murmured into the phone and followed up quickly with an agreement in case he'd heard it.

He was already there, a drink in hand, immersed in a pile of documents and immune apparently to the relaxed atmosphere and the music. When he looked up, Lacey was extremely satisfied with his mini double-take. She had gone to some trouble to achieve just that. After all, there was no point in being a designer if she couldn't at least contrive to make Luke Harrow look twice. Even once would be an improvement.

She'd organised it like a campaign. If she was to get anywhere with this job Mr Harrow had first to register her as an entity. Green silk, she'd decided upon. Austere style—high neck, three-quarter sleeves—absolutely no suggestion of suggestiveness at all—*but* it had a certain un-puritan cling about it that suited her more than adequate figure. Nothing of the robot there, she'd thought when she dressed. Hair—an uncomprisingly business-like style, pulled back in a knob and no frills. Of course, it was a natural, streaky blonde and looked good that way as she well knew. Her only jewellery was a heavy antique gold chain and a jade set ring. Her bag—a geometric patterned envelope tucked under one arm, her shoes plain, glamour-cut, stiletto-heeled. 'Style,' her first employer had said of her in the days when she couldn't afford silk or jewellery. 'That's what you've got, duckie, and it'll take you a long way.'

As Luke Harrow unwound from his chair and Lacey held out a hand to him she hoped her 'style' would shake off that first unfortunate impression she'd made. If, of course, she'd made any at all.

'Good evening, Mr Harrow.' His hand engulfed hers. A brief pressure and he let it drop.

'Miss Teale.' He had the name all right now, she thought as his blue eyes wandered over her face and shoulders. She widened her smile, wondering why he looked now and hadn't bothered the other day. Maybe her own mental meanderings had made her appear shy or hesitant and therefore easily overlooked. His eyes stayed on her face and she was satisfied that she had registered as a person this time. She had used her make-up for more effect tonight, blending a touch of the exotic with her usual crisp effect. Her generous mouth was glossed with a warm brandy coral and her cheekbones touched with blusher. But now that she'd got his attention, she had to hold it. As they sat down she said:

'You must forgive me, Mr Harrow, if I seemed a little vague at our first meeting. Unfortunately I've been under some pressure lately. I do apologise.'

She was fully aware that there was no note of apology in her words at all. What she was really saying was 'forget the doormat you met yesterday—here is the real Lacey Teale, Decorator'. He got the message.

'You don't look at all vague tonight, Miss Teale,' he murmured, stacking up his papers with economical moves of his shapely hands. 'Would you like a drink?'

'Thank you. A Campari.'

He passed the order on, put away his paperwork in a slim case and leaned back, the sportsman's lines of his body apparent beneath the unbuttoned charcoal suit jacket. There was a square definition to his jaw now that had been less obvious in any of her pin-ups of him, and lines cut vertically into his cheeks. His mouth wore the perpetual curve of the cynic and his eyes were cool, guarded. But he was immensely attractive for all that. Maybe even more than he had been in his golden days when her schoolfriends had dubbed him 'too nice' to moon over. Now with an air of 'don't give a damn' in the set of his formidable shoulders, the touch of mystery in the shuttered, once-candid blue eyes Luke Harrow was intriguing. Lacey thrust her glasses on more securely. He was a client. And clients could be interesting, boring, friendly . . . *never* intriguing.

'Have you ever hired a decorator before, Mr Harrow?'

He thrust out his lower lip and shook his head. One hand swirled the drink in his glass and the ice cubes clinked against the straight sides.

'Perhaps I should explain to you then, just how we—— '

'We?' He shot out. Lacey pressed her lips together. She would have to get used to these monosyllabic bullets she supposed. After a promising start he seemed to have regressed. Her jaw tensed. But Mr Harrow wasn't going to start treating her like a robot again, not if she could help it.

'My partner—Mike Logan—and myself,' she explained with a brilliant smile. 'We like to get to know our clients, understand their lifestyle, their special interests, tastes—so that we can formulate something that is only partly us and mostly you. . . .'

Her drink came and she sipped it, giving him the opportunity to make some answer. None came and she forged on, professionally pleasant. 'Of course, in your case we already know a little about your special interests—— ' This reference to his previous fame as a tennis player went unremarked. Her lips firmed. Of course, she could equally be referring to his other apparent special interest. Women. Luke Harrow might avoid the press, refuse to give interviews or even brief statements about his current protégés, but he didn't stop them photographing him with the women he escorted. Maybe it was a game he played with them in subtle revenge for their condemnation of him so long ago. For though he attracted their attention by attending premières and charity balls with eye-catching women, the most he ever said was 'no comment'. Was it through one of his well-heeled girlfriends that he'd come across her work?

'The purpose of this preliminary meeting is to—allow for some—— ' Darn it, she thought furiously, why was it so hard to say the well-worn words to this man? He simply sat back in his chair, watching her over his glass and listening intently. But contributing nothing.

'—discussion on your needs, for us to toss around a few ideas——' She began to feel she was talking him into it. As if he hadn't been the one who had phoned and requested her services. Several other openings for comment passed in silence. Maybe he had a hearing problem.

'And the first thing I need to know is just which room or rooms you want us to handle for you?' There now. A direct question. The man couldn't ignore that.

'I thought I'd made that clear at the start. All of them, Miss Teale.'

Lacey put her glass on the table with great deliberation. She didn't remember him saying so and she would be unlikely to forget such a bombshell. There were bigger in Sydney itself of course, but Fremont must be one of the largest houses of its style in the Camden-Picton region.

'All of them?' she repeated. 'You mean—the house will be empty—all of it—and you want us to design the entire layout?'

'Not empty entirely. But I will want you to look at every room, yes. You seem surprised, Miss Teale. Is the job within your capabilities?'

She bridled a little at his tone. 'I think so, Mr Harrow. But to be quite frank with you, I have to admit that I personally have not worked on a project of this size before.' It would almost be a relief if he found that fact off-putting and cancelled the whole thing. The treacherous thought startled her. Throw away possibly the biggest job of their careers because of some vague personal disquiet about the man? But the more she experienced his steady regard and her own peculiar spine-tingling awareness, the more she was convinced that this could be a mistake.

'That's honest of you,' he remarked, dry as dust, and she clenched her fingers about her glass again. Well, she thought, normal courtesy and big smiles had got her nowhere. Perhaps it was time for a bit of plain speaking.

'I'm always honest with clients, Mr Harrow. Sometimes I have to be painfully honest and I'm going to be just that now.'

The blue eyes narrowed on her in surprise at her directness.

'Mr Harrow, when clients contact us—me—regarding a job to be done, I usually enjoy some exchange of information with them. Rarely do I have to prise details from people who have already decided freely to have work done on their homes. Mr Harrow—I am not a saleswoman trying to sell you an insurance policy you don't want, or a set of encyclopaedias.'

There seemed no change in his expression and Lacey's eyes sparkled with anger. She whipped off her glasses and leaned forward. At least she had his full attention. That was something. 'If you don't want to talk to me, Mr Harrow, I see no point in us going any further. I cannot work in a vacuum and refuse to simply do as some decorators do and make a bulk buy of suitable reproduction furniture, match up the carpets and the curtains, toss in a truckload of ornaments and present you with a whopping great bill!'

There was a silence. Not just from Luke but from the closer tables too, where her rising voice had carried. Boy—she had done it now. Mike was going to be rightly furious about this. Her plain speaking had somehow turned to temper. He glanced around. Heads that were turned towards them instantly swung away again. Lacey took a deep breath, closed her eyes for a few seconds in a mix of mortification at losing her temper and lingering anger with the man. She had probably created a new record. Most clients remained on their books longer than two days. But when she looked again, he was smiling. Nothing too extravagant—just a stretching of those well-cut lips, but it was enough to add another dimension to Lacey's discomposure. To her dismay she heard the tripped beat of her heart and a quick pounding in her ears. Get a grip on yourself, Lacey—you're not fourteen anymore.

He didn't even bother with a reply. The waiter came over and he nudged her menu towards her, 'Have you decided yet what you'd like to eat, Miss Teale?'

'No,' she snapped from the depths of confusion. He held her eyes for long seconds until she put on her glasses again and made a quick choice from the menu. When the waiter had taken the order and gone, her client murmured: 'Do you have to wear glasses all the time?' And it was so unexpected that she stammered.

'Oh—um. Yes.' she finished firmly. Mike was right. On this occasion at least she was hiding behind them. But from what, she couldn't say.

'Hmm. Pity. It occurs to me that I owe you an apology, Miss Teale. You are quite right. I've been surly.'

'I didn't say that,' she intervened quickly, astonished at this turnabout.

'Perish the thought,' he smiled. 'As if you'd accuse a client of being surly. You're *much* too tactful for that.'

'That's a subtle reprimand if ever I heard one,' Lacey eyed him with wariness.

'Subtlety is not my strong point, Miss Teale, as you're likely to discover. I apologise for my abruptness the other day and—tonight. I've had something rather . . . something on my mind. You've set my fears to rest actually. There's always the chance that even a talented professional like yourself might be wooed from integrity by the prospect of a well-paid project. I'm relieved to know that you wouldn't do a token job for the cash involved.'

'Did you set me up just to establish that?' she demanded and took off the glasses again. He studied the result with interest. Lacey felt warm suddenly.

'Not exactly. I often work on the principle of letting the other person do all the talking. In the end they usually tell me what I'd never hear otherwise. Your little outburst was reassuring.'

'Is that so? Well let me tell you, Mr Harrow, that there's one thing I said in my "little outburst" that I *will* do.'

'What's that?' the deep voice sharpened.

'Whatever else happens—I'll present you with a whopping great bill!'

He tossed back his head and laughed and Lacey watched the years peel away. Her stomach did a lazy roll over and her head, her so sensible, man-hardened head, sent out a weak little warning. Just for a few moments he was the young man again—his smile charming, his good humour magnetic. What am I getting into, she thought as her stomach lurched a second time. Her eyes were glued to this devastating man and as he stopped laughing she shifted her gaze and put on her glasses. With her forefinger she stabbed them on more firmly.

Somehow she had the feeling she had just made a transparent gesture.

His smile was faintly mocking as if he too thought so. But just for a moment she saw the look in his eyes—a look of awakened interest that had the professional in her disapproving, and the woman—excited. And wary.

'Tell me—do you have a favourite colour that might influence your furnishings?'

He looked at her a long time 'There is a colour,' he said. 'A green. Not one of those overpowering emeralds or jades—more of a——' he searched around the restaurant's burgundy and gold colour scheme then looked back at her. Before she could chart his movement he reached over and tipped her glasses down on to her nose, '—a sea green with a flash of gold here and there.'

Their gazes held, then Lacey pushed the frames back with the quick gesture that had become second nature.

'I see.' Her voice was quite level. Inside she felt a tremor of something new, unidentifiable. He's a client, she repeated to herself. A client. 'Green and gold. A popular combination for the marbling effects often used in houses of Fremont's vintage . . .' she went on sounding pompous even to her own ears, but rattled by the trend of this meeting. She might have done better to remain the miracle robot he'd expected. When she had set out to change that image of herself with him, she hadn't counted on a heavy swing from cold to warm. Lacey went into unnecessary detail on colour and glazes as applied to Australian Victorian houses, conscious that now she had his fullest attention.

'You seem to know a bit about Fremont, Miss Teale,' he remarked when she had moved from the general to the specific.

'Only hearsay and photographs. I've never been inside. But I was born in the district. My parents still live nearby. We used to drive to a picnic place on the river when I was a child and I always looked for "The Big House". Fremont has been something of a landmark in the area ever since it was built I should think.'

His mouth tensed. 'Yes, I've noticed the gawpers already.'

'Surely you wouldn't expect anything else, Mr Harrow?'

'What do you mean?'

'Well—the house itself has a certain shabby, bygone glamour that attracts attention and now *you* own it, so——' she shrugged, aware of having expressed it badly.

'And the owner matches the house—is that what you're trying to say?'

She flicked a glance over his handsome, disillusioned features, the strong neck, the sportsman's shoulders. 'No, Mr Harrow. Shabby, bygone glamour is *not* the way I would describe you.'

He smiled and lost years from his face. 'I think I'll take that as a compliment.' There was a glint in the blue eyes that had her reminding herself of the nature of this meeting. This is business. Get on with it, Lacey.

'Are you intending to restore the house, Mr Harrow— or do your alterations take the form of improvements?'

'There's a fine line between both, surely,' he lifted his wine glass, regarded her over it. 'Or is there? Suppose you tell me, Miss Teale.'

It was irresistible of course and Lacey saddled her hobby horse and galloped on, pausing only for him to order coffee.

'My feeling,' she finished up, 'is that wherever possible, the character and the—integrity of houses like Fremont should be respected. Preserved.' Somewhat embarrassed by her fervour she stopped in another of his silences and was impelled to add, 'Your entrance hall for instance. I believe it is superb and it would be a pity to just modernise something so individual.'

Another of those long pauses. Lacey fiddled with her almost empty glass. Luke Harrow's mood appeared to have swung about to gloomy.

'As it happens I agree with you. But I'm afraid Fremont's entrance will need a little more than restoration. Reconstruction more like. It has been damaged in a fire.'

'Fire?' she was dismayed. 'But when? How much damage?'

'The night before last,' he clipped. Was that the weight on his mind that had made him so snappy? 'Fortunately I was there and able to stop it before it went too far. A few crates full of personal effects that had arrived from storage were damaged. And the timber—er——' he held out a hand to indicate waist height.

'Dado?'

'That's it. Some of it has been destroyed. The glass panels beside the front door exploded but the surrounds might be saved. Bartlett, an architect, is looking at them for me.'

'Owen Bartlett?'

He nodded.

'In that case Fremont is in good hands,' she smiled. 'How did the fire start?'

He closed up instantly, shuttering even the shutters he kept on his inmost thoughts. 'I've no idea.'

'But you said you were in the house at the time——'

'Yes.' The word snapped out, an unmistakable finial and Lacey obeyed prudence and didn't pursue the matter. But her early uneasiness about him increased. There was something unnaturally secretive about him. It went far beyond the yen for privacy that was perfectly understandable in a man who had had his every move photographed and commented upon from the age of sixteen, when he'd won the Junior Titles crown.

This preliminary meeting must be the most unproductive she had ever experienced. Even though Luke Harrow was talking now he was telling her little. Every avenue she trod down came to a dead end with him.

How, she asked herself, was she going to even begin this massive task?

'Mr Harrow—you haven't told me anything yet,' she blurted out with unaccustomed lack of finesse. 'About yourself. What you expect to *do* in your house—entertain—work? Lock yourself away——?' Again her words were ill chosen but he didn't freeze up this time.

'Lock myself away,' he repeated with a gruff laugh. 'Not that at least. I tried that years ago and it doesn't work.' He stood up and held out a hand to her. 'Come and dance with me, Miss Teale.'

She blinked at the tall figure looming over her.

'Dance? Mr Harrow, this is a business meeting. I came here to learn something about you and your expectations.'

'Then dance with me and you might learn some of them.'

There was something in his tone. Something.

'How could dancing have the faintest connection with my work on your house?'

He bent and placed both hands flat on the table, looked thoughtfully into her face.

'There *is* the ballroom,' he suggested with a twitch of his lips.

So his sense of humour hadn't atrophied. Lacey looked up into quizzical blue eyes and almost wished it had. Already she was far too drawn to the man in spite of his moodiness. She had to forget those old photos and this new flesh-and-blood image and think of him as the biggest cheque Logan and Teale were likely to get.

'All right. You win,' she smiled.

As she turned to face him on the dance floor, she met his eyes briefly. It was only a dance. The necessary physical contacts didn't mean a thing. Nevertheless she found herself hard pushed to remember she was merely obliging the whim of a client when he put a hand to the small of her back. Client! she thought, in renewed amazement. This was Luke Harrow, the man who had filled her adolescent head with fantasies. She nearly laughed. Dancing in his arms had been a favourite fantasy at fourteen. How different real life was from girlish dreams.

Gingerly she rested her fingertips on his shoulder and focused on anything beyond him while she framed a few work-orientated questions she could ask to the romantic Latin jazz of the band.

'Relax,' he urged her and jogged his hand at her waist, 'I won't seduce you,' and as her eyes flew startled to his, he added, 'not here.'

CHAPTER TWO

THERE was an obvious answer to that and Lacey almost made it. Instead she looked at him and said blandly: 'May I ask how you came to choose Logan and Teale, Mr Harrow?'

There was an appreciative gleam in his eyes. 'Very deft recovery, Miss Teale.'

'You were the one who was wrong-footed.'

'Was I?'

To her dismay she couldn't hold that warm, caressing gaze. He smiled when she glanced away. There was more than one way of seducing a woman she thought, and Luke Harrow doubtless knew them all. In vain she searched for a courteous, crushing rejoinder but he went on smoothly: 'A—friend of mine has a flat at Darling Point and she told me you'd decorated it for her. I like it.'

Her brain raced through her files of Darling Point jobs. A woman friend of Luke Harrow ... she rejected elegant Mrs Raneleigh on the grounds of age, Mrs Dawson because there had been a besotted Mr Dawson. ... The brunette. Annette Cromer—plunge-necked pantsuits and all the necessary equipment to fill them. She seemed a likely friend for Mr Harrow. Etruscan red walls, she thought, remembering the assignment, and a Blackman original and a ghastly round bed that Ms Cromer had insisted on keeping. ...

Luke Harrow related one or two details about the Cromer layout that had pleased him and Lacey filed the information away. He didn't mention the round bed.

'I've never come across your partner's work.'

'Mike's very good. Especially in the contemporary field.'

'And what's your special field, Miss Teale?'

'Oh, I've made my name in——' she paused, reluctant suddenly to make the old joke.

'Yes? In——?' he prompted with a malicious grin that made her think he already knew very well. After all, her bedroom series had just been given publicity in a prominent glossy magazine.

'Bedrooms,' she finished shortly.

'Ah. What luck.' His hand pressed more persuasively on her back, slipped a fraction over the silk and moved her closer to him.

'Why do you say that?'

'I'm very interested in bedrooms too.' He clasped her hand warmly, propelled her closer still under the pretext of a turn to the music, so that she brushed against the fabric of his suit, felt the intimate touch of his thighs.

'Yes, I know, Mr Harrow,' she said dryly thinking of Annette Cromer and the others. 'I did say that we already knew of your special interests.'

Blue eyes, just inches from her, held her gaze steadily. His lips tilted at the corners.

'You have claws, Miss Teale.'

'It's a necessity, Mr Harrow.'

'Even with clients.'

'Especially with clients.'

'Even with clients who will end up paying a "whopping great bill"?'

'Even with those,' she returned gravely, trying to ignore the sheer exhilaration that raced through her body, prompted by the small, warm contacts with him and the verbal sparring which seemed just an extension of this physical communication. His mouth parted in a smile and so close, she saw the strong, white teeth attractively uneven—one minutely chipped in a freak on-court accident at Forest Hills. How incredible to think that long ago, when she had been a leggy fourteen, she had watched it happen on television—watched the tall, muscular young God of the court grin engagingly afterwards for the cameras to show the damage. And here she was now—in his arms with a bird's eye view.

'In fact my interest is quite valid as I've so recently acquired six bedrooms. Your expertise in each of them will be most valuable.'

It was said dead-pan. He was baiting her she realised, to

see how much she was prepared to take from a top client.

'I'm flattered that you should say so, Mr Harrow. And tell me, are you planning on having a trophy room?'

He leaned back, looked into her face. 'For my tennis trophies you mean?'

'Wide-eyed she looked back, 'Well, of course, Mr Harrow. What else?'

His laugh was quick, low. 'Call me Luke.'

'If you want me to. Call me Lacey.'

'Lacey,' he murmured.

The music slowed, scarcely moving them on the dance floor. Their movements were relaxed, well matched. Almost familiar.

'I have the feeling that I might get you interested in my bedrooms, Lacey——'

The last distance between them vanished. Lacey was held hard against him and no matter how she tried she couldn't stiffen her muscles. Traitorously her body refused even to remain passive, moving subtly to the shape of his. To deny his effect would be futile. A piece of dishonesty that could only be coy.

'Possibly, Luke. But you'd have the devil's own job getting me into the trophy room.'

His laughter vibrated through her, conveyed through his chest and diaphragm and he put his cheek against hers. Into her ear he said: 'But that's what they call me—didn't you know. The tarnished golden boy— the Saint Luke of the press, turned devil. When you come to Fremont, Lacey, you'll be in the devil's court.' His tone turned sour.

'Can you be that bad, Luke?'

'Of course I'm that bad. Would the press ever lie?' he said sardonically.

Whatever train of thought she had set up, it effectively slowed the rather dizzying trend of the evening and Lacey's relief was pierced by an arrow of regret. But they left the dance floor and settled down to a discussion that was much more what she had expected.

'The next step is for you to come to Fremont and see the renovations. The house is half full of furniture that I want integrated into the whole.' She kept her face carefully expressionless at that. How many times had she been to look at the furniture much loved by fond owners, only to find it virtually impossible to design around. In fact her reputation had been built on just that ability. To integrate the impossible with the impeccable. But not without enormous difficulty.

'Much of it belonged to my parents and theirs before them and some of it I bought myself,' he explained with a half smile. 'And it is good. Not a truckload of reproductions I assure you.'

She really would have to tread carefully. Luke Harrow was reading her like a book.

He went into detail about his plans for the house. The unusually large tract of land around it—trimmed only slightly from its original size—was to become his second tennis ranch. Two courts were completed and others already under construction. Gardens had been planted between them and the house's gracious neglected environs. The old stables and outbuildings were to be converted to accommodation for players.

'And there would be a coach house I imagine. What are your plans for it?'

'Why—it'll serve its original purpose,' he grinned, 'and house the coach.'

She laughed.

'And of course for VIP guests who might want a few weeks practice and respite from the press—a couple of the house's guest bedrooms will be kept available.' Judging by his hard jaw there would be no place a publicity weary player would be more likely to keep his privacy than at Fremont.

'Then there's my mother. She has a suite of rooms that give her privacy from the rest of the house.'

Mother? Lacey was startled. Somehow with his double talk about his bedrooms and trophies she hadn't pictured him living with his mother.

'Yes, I do have one you know. So you can come to Fremont secure in the knowledge that you have a chaperone.' His mouth twisted as he said it and she was curious to know the reason. There was a great deal unsaid in every word Luke uttered, she decided.

'I'm not sure that it makes me feel safe at all,' she admitted, surprised at her own candidness. She was not normally given to dissembling, but neither was she so ready to admit her feelings.

'You're a very percipient woman, Lacey.' He looked at her keenly, 'And an honest one.'

'Not usually so honest. Not——'

'——on the first date?' he supplied mockingly.

'Not on such short acquaintance. And this isn't a date, Luke. It's a business meeting.' She raised her hand and the waiter came over. 'Could I have the bill please?' she asked, much to Luke's amusement.

'This is a treat for me. I'm not often wined and dined by a career woman who pays the bill.'

But when the account came, Luke pinned her wrist to the table with one hand and slipped his other into his jacket for his wallet.

'Luke, please. This is to go on my expense account.'

'Not tonight.'

'But I expected to pay.'

'You will,' he said softly. 'But not tonight.'

On the way out, he ignored the stares of those who recognised him, nodded impassively to the waiter who opened the door for them. He unlocked the door of the white Alfa Romeo parked close to the entrance and tossed his document case inside it and slammed the door. Lacey held out her hand.

'Goodnight, Luke. Shall I phone you again for a suitable time to visit Fremont?' Her hand wavered. He didn't take it.

'I'll ring you,' he said. 'Your home phone number is on the card you left with me yesterday. Is it—convenient to ring you there?' One eyebrow went up eloquently.

She caught the unframed question. 'What you mean is—am I living with someone?'

'Are you?'

'Well, yes, as a matter of fact—but ring anyway,' she smiled.

'What's her name?'

'What makes you think my flatmate is a girl?'

The lighting out here was paltry but Lacey saw the teasing glint in his eyes. 'You just aren't the type for live-in lovers—it shows in your eyes. I could almost feel it when we danced——'

She gave a snort of amusement. He didn't believe any such thing but her spine tingled that he should be so carelessly accurate. '—besides, I rang tonight to change our meeting place, but you'd already left. A girl answered the phone.'

He chuckled and walked with her to her car. Lacey laughed with him. 'That doesn't prove anything. She might just have been visiting me and my—flatmate.'

'Was she?'

They were at her car and Luke leaned an arm on it, inclined his head towards her for her answer. Lacey had a hand in her bag, withdrawing her keys, but was held still by the quality of waiting in him. He really wanted to know. It was none of his business what her domestic arrangements were. She wouldn't tell him. She stared into his eyes. There were two tiny points of light in them—reflections of the parking area's fluorescent lights. Over behind him a car backed out, it's tailights blinking red, its radio throwing a snatch of rock music across to them, before it drove away. A cool August breeze blew. Lacey was warm. Very warm.

'No, you're right,' she said to her own surprise. 'I share with her.' He moved and she dragged out her keys in a rush and a released jangle—her words came out the same way.

'Well, goodnight, Luke. It's been a——' But the keys dropped from her fingers and her voice stopped on an indrawn breath. For Luke's arm was around her waist and his hand was curved to her nape. The pin-points of light drew nearer and her bag followed the keys to the ground as she held on to him for balance, one hand slipping beneath his jacket.

'Luke—don't——' she said as he removed her glasses. But the words were lost beneath his mouth. Her fingers spread against his ribs—spread and pushed for just a moment, but there was a seducing warmth to the soft fabric that slipped a little over steel-hard muscle,

and instead she clung. And though she twisted her head
she only succeeded in turning his lips to her cheek along
her jaw's clear line to the hollow of her neck . . . his warm
breath fanned through green silk, and the touch of it was a
sorcery against which she had no defence. When he put
his mouth to hers again Lacey's control slipped away—a
rush of bubbles escaping upwards through her body. Her
lips relaxed, shaped to his, so perfectly moulded that she
could almost believe he was withdrawing the word 'no'
from her mouth. In her mind she could hear an
affirmative forming. Arms around him, her body was
already saying yes. Another car started up, revved its
motor then stalled. When it started again in reluctant
hoops, Lacey tore herself away, remembering too late the
things she'd told herself all evening. Luke's hand lingered
at her waist and he looked down wordlessly at her. Then
he reached up and took her glasses from the roof of the car
and slipped them on to her nose.

'It's a start,' he murmured. 'You took them off for a
few minutes and look what happened. Be warned,
Lacey—I want to see them off all night——'

He almost whispered the last words. Like a promise.
Lacey had a swift vision of a massive bed, curtained
and plump with pillows and herself on it with Luke. . . .

'I didn't take them off, Luke. You did.'

'Ah—but what a challenge to get you to take them
off voluntarily.' He laughed and ran an index finger
down the side of her face.

'Don't think of me as a challenge, Luke. You might
have won your opening game but that was because . . . I
wasn't prepared. I'm not going to be another trophy.
And I'm not one of those women who might consider
sleeping with Luke Harrow a kind of trophy either.'

'Oh damn!' he said softly. 'I was hoping you might
want me for my body.'

Unsteadily she laughed as she got into the car.

'It is very nice of course, but I want you for your
floors and windows and hallways.' Not a bad riposte
for a girl shaken to the roots of her being.

'And bedrooms,' he said wickedly at the window and
tossed her bag on to her lap before she drove away.

'So you're decorating for Luke Harrow himself,' her flatmate grinned when Lacey let herself in. 'Tell me, is he really as sexy as he sounds on the phone?'

'I wouldn't know,' Lacey said lightly, reluctant to talk about Luke to Beth or anyone else just yet. Until she'd re-played tonight to herself and analysed it. 'I only had dinner with him. But if you like, next time I see him—I'll ask.'

Beth giggled and searched around on the floor for something in her sewing muddle of paper patterns and fabric. 'That might be asking for the kind of trouble you don't go in for,' she said, and stuck a number of pins in her mouth when she failed to find the tin. 'According to the rumours, he isn't the nice boy he used to be—and with those looks and that voice he could be a very dangerous animal.'

It came out 'a vewy dangewouf animaw' through the pins and Lacey smiled, but said nothing. In a minute her friend looked at her and asked with difficulty, 'Well? How did the dinner go with him and why didn't you tell me it was *him* you were seeing tonight?'

'Hmmm?' Lacey pushed at her glasses with her index finger and blinked. 'Oh, I didn't think to mention it. He wants us to do his entire house—a Victorian mansion. Our biggest job to date.'

'Wow!' Beth dropped pins from her mouth and put them back. 'What a pity he hates publicity so much— you might never get your gorgeous interiors photographed for the women's glossies.'

'No, but he intends to have guests at the house, so we should get a few word-of-mouth referrals in time.' She lapsed into thought again and Beth eyed her.

'Lacey—something wrong?'

'Just thinking about all that work,' she lied in the face of Beth's curiousity, 'Luke wants his job done by the end of summer and I've got several others *and* Mrs Prentiss' penthouse to do. You remember what Mrs Prentiss was like when we did her mountain cottage don't you? Pink, pink and more pink and never quite the shade she wanted.'

'Get your curly headed partner to attend to Mrs

Prentiss. You're always telling me what a way he has with women.'

'Anyone would think you don't like Mike.' Lacey smiled. It was only six months since they'd begun sharing, but Beth had met Mike countless times. Enough to get to like him. Everyone liked Mike. So Lacey was taken aback when Beth gave a wry grin and made a see-saw motion with one hand.

'He's so-so, I guess.' But her quick look away sent Lacey to the bathroom wondering if Beth was being quite honest. In her own efforts to be honest she forgot about Beth, and tried instead to analyse what had happened tonight. Harrowing, she thought soberly, giving it up. She had known all long he would be difficult. There were just a few details she'd got wrong.

The next morning she had to go over it again with Mike.

'Fremont is such a big house that I'll have to see it before I can do another thing,' she explained. 'He has it partly furnished and I can only hope that the stuff he has is okay. Somehow,' she thought of Luke's restrained taste in clothes, his choice of restaurant, wine, 'I think it will be. He doesn't seem to have spent the last years just keeping his muscles in trim.'

'And are they?'

'Are they what?'

'In trim. His muscles.' Mike flicked shrewd eyes to her face and she made an elaborate fluttering of her lashes.

'Ooooh yes—supah!' she drooled, then: 'Really, Mike, I wasn't checking out his muscles. He seemed a bit easier to get along with last night . . .' she baulked on the understatement and changed tack abruptly.

'Just think of it, the *whole* house, partner. And from what I can gather, his budget isn't going to be exactly cheese-paring. I can hardly wait to start,' she said, genuine enthusiasm making her eyes shine. Fremont, quite apart from the intentions of its owner, was a challenge. Or was she being naive to think she could keep them apart?

'Our accountant will be delighted. So am I, Lacey.

That goes without saying. But is it the house or its owner that's putting that colour in your face?'

'You're as bad as Beth,' Lacey exclaimed. 'Trying to make something out of nothing. She went on about me having dinner with him—as if it's unusual for me to dine with a client.'

'Does she know you used to have a crush on him?'

'No. And I'm heartily sorry I ever told *you* that. It was when I was fourteen for heaven's sake, Mike. I'm a big girl now.'

He grinned. 'That's what I keep telling you. How about coming up to my pad after work today, big girl? You could scrub my back for me and then——'

She smiled, shook her head and he sighed. 'No? All right then, what about a bit of Rachmaninov and Stroganoff——' he eyed her well-curved figure in its classic suit, '—and, of course, hands off.'

Lacey began to feel uncomfortable again. Her few dates with Mike had been a mistake. Not that they hadn't been enjoyable, but they had introduced a new element into their hitherto excellent working arrangement, an element she'd been trying to eliminate ever since.

'No, sorry. Beth's got something special planned for dinner tonight. She bought a new cookbook.' It was half true, she thought guiltily, though the book had been a gift for someone else. Mike looked sceptical about Beth's ability with a cookbook.

'It beats me how you can put up with that girl. She doesn't seem to have a brain in her head and your place is always ankle deep in her possessions.'

'It's not *my* place, it's *ours*. And Beth has more brains than you think and heaps of personality. And she's darned good looking too,' she added on impulse. Mike inclined his head towards one shoulder.

'She's so-so, I suppose,' he relented, and it amused Lacey that he used the same words that Beth had about him. Interesting . . . '—but not my type at all.' Mike finished.

'Dear—dear—she *will* be shattered when I tell her that,' Lacey said. 'No, perhaps I shouldn't. She might throw herself over The Gap if she's told that the talented, the charismatic Mike Logan doesn't fancy her!'

'Okay, I get the message. I'm not my sunny self today. I didn't mean any disrespect to your flatmate.'

'You two have more in common than you think, as a matter of fact.' Lacey smiled and slit open another envelope from their pile of mail. Mike threw her a darkling look and went to answer his phone, muttering his usual promises to 'hire a full-time secretary one of these days'. They made do with part-time help and an answering service right now.

'After the Harrow job, we might be able to,' she called to him and just saying the name tripped her heartbeat and jerked the paperknife in her hand.

Fortunately Mike was not there when Luke phoned. Nor was Sandra, their part-time typist. For Lacey removed her glasses at the sound of his voice and knew that her smile was like no other she'd ever had for a client either on the telephone or off.

'Good afternoon, Luke,' she said formally, but her pleasure in hearing him must have communicated along the wires.

'You're smiling,' he said. 'I can tell.'

She could believe it. He was smiling back at her. It was in those honey-brown tones. Lacey grabbed her glasses and put them on again. Crazy!

'I imagine you're ringing to make a date for me to come to Fremont, Luke——'

'Oh—oh. You've put those glasses on again, haven't you?'

Her hand went nervously to them. 'How did you——? I had them on all the time,' she lied, wondering how he'd known.

'No,' he said softly. 'You sound different without them.'

Of course she had to ask. 'How do I sound?'

'Softer . . . less fortressed.'

She laughed. 'Fortressed! Oh, Luke, surely not?'

'I'm exaggerating.' That smile was in his voice again, tilting that handsome broad-cut mouth, and she could conjure up the look of it in his eyes.

'Luke——' she began, pushing at her glasses. He broke in.

'I know, I know—we should be talking about curtains or something.'

'Well, you *are* a client.'

'Tonight I don't want to talk about colours or wallpaper designs. Do you like fish and chips?'

Her heart gave a couple of extra beats. 'Yes—but *never* on a paper. I loathe those cute still-life designs.'

He gave a low chuckle. 'Share some with me tonight, Lacey? Fish and chips, not wallpaper.'

'I——' she tussled with her rule of non-fraternisation with the clients which had already been weakened by her flirting last night.

'You owe me a dinner,' he added. 'Tonight *you* pay.'

She laughed at that. 'How would that look on my expenses budget? Fish and chips with a Very Important Client?'

'Not a client. Not tonight. And I was kidding about paying. Let me pick you up. Where do you live?'

'That's not necessary,' she managed to say. Her head was spinning as he swept her into agreement. For she knew she would agree. 'I'll meet you. Where?'

'Circular Quay then. The Manly wharf. Around seven?'

Long after she hung up she stared at the phone, aware of having taken an unprecedented step. Already she had overstepped the barrier she maintained between herself and those for whom she worked. That kiss last night was bad enough and now here she was itching to meet him. She looked at her watch. It was only four-fifteen. Nearly three hours. Lacey returned impatiently to her work and tried to remember when she had clock-watched in her seven-year career. And no amount of concentration could evade the answer. Never.

She locked up and left before Mike came back, walking eagerly to Oxford Street and wishing that today she had her car. Two buses and an awesome Harbour Bridge traffic snarl later, she dashed into her flat and breathlessly explained to Beth that she was eating out tonight.

'With your perfectionist partner I suppose,' Beth said with a certain stiffness about her mouth.

'Perfectionist?'

'He always looks at me as if I'm something the dog dragged in, just because I'm a bit untidy.'

Lacey laughed. 'It's Luke Harrow if you must know.'

Beth blinked in surprise. 'Is it business?'

'Mostly.'

'You won't be out of your depth there will you, Lacey? I mean Luke Harrow—he's——'

'I know. A "vewy dangewouf animaw".' Lacey grinned. She rang for a cab. In record time she showered, changed into jeans, a sweater and a cord jacket. She left her hair loose and her glasses on. Beth looked askance at her sneakers.

'Must be a very casual dinner.'

'In the light of your warning I thought I should wear my running shoes.' She replied and left.

He was waiting. In a roll-neck sweater and jeans he strolled by a closed snack bar, paused to look at a paperback stand outside a news kiosk. In his left hand swung a black BYO insulated container. He looked boyishly handsome but tense. Lacey quickened her pace to reach him, slowed the last few steps as he saw her. His face lit with his smile and its welcome bowled her over. Putting up a hand to her glasses, she stayed at a distance. 'I'm sorry I'm late,' she said with a certain breathlessness. From the long walk along the Quay, that was all, she told herself.

'You're here,' he replied as if that was all that mattered. 'And I expected to wait. I always do for a woman,' he added cheerfully. He gave her an odd look then as if he hadn't meant to say that, but she was rather glad he had. It reminded her that it was, after all, only the second time she'd met him—that initial interview could be discounted entirely—and any idea that this informal date meant something special was unfounded. She was just another attractive woman to Luke. As she moved closer to his side and walked with him she told herself that it was enough for the moment.

'What's your limit?' she enquired. 'How long do you wait before you give up?'

'Ah. That depends on the woman. For some I'd wait—mmm—as long as ten minutes.'

'Do you mean if I'd been another three minutes getting here, you would have gone?' she said lightly.

'For you I could have stretched a point,' he told her, and put a hand to her waist to guide her past the Manly wharf.

'I'll bet you say that to all the girls,' she said weakly at this sudden closeness. 'Where are we going?'

'I see you've got your walking shoes on, so how about a stroll to the Opera House?'

The Quay's winds were as blustery as ever, roughing up the dark water that slapped about stanchions and sea-walls. Lacey's hair was in a tangle before they reached the Opera House forecourt but she let it blow, not bothering to hold it back. They walked around Bennelong Point where the big, sailed building seemed to sit almost in the water itself. The wind swept their words away, so they did not speak much and words, in any case, seemed superfluous. Near the majestic main entrance, men in dinner jackets and diamond-clustered women stood drinking champagne from long-stemmed glasses.

'Ah, this is the place.' Luke urged her to sit on the steps between the élite groups of patrons. He grinned at her surprise and opened his insulated pack to produce a bottle of white wine, a corkscrew and two plastic cups.

'Here?' she said, looking around as he put a disposable cup in her hand.

'The perfect place for pre-dinner drinks,' he assured her and poured the wine. 'Do you want to make a toast to the Opera House?'

'No. Utzon has said everything that needs to be said.' She waved a hand at the soaring, spot-lit arches and curves.

'You like it then?'

She nodded. 'I like the outside better than the inside.' After a sip of wine she added, 'Sour grapes.'

He grinned, 'The wine?'

'No. The Opera House interior. I wasn't even *asked* to submit *my* ideas.'

'You were a babe in arms at the time—or a gleam in your father's eye.'

'So *that's* the reason!' She snapped her fingers and giggled, earning a snooty look from a nearby pearl-encrusted matron. They stayed there to finish their drink, two jeaned gatecrashers.

'It's not fair. They've paid a small fortune to drink champers here before the performance and here we are doing it on the cheap with a BYO outfit and plastic cups. And having just as much——' she paused, eyes wide on his.

'Fun?' he finished, and put the bottle and cups in the pack again. He held her arm as they began descending the steps. 'I took a risk. You might have hated doing it on the cheap.'

'Luke, I didn't mean that as a criticism.'

'I know you didn't.' His fingers slipped down her arm and gripped her hand. 'Most girls, believe it or not, hate picnics on the Opera House steps. But you,' his hand moved on hers, his fingers pleasantly warm and strong, 'you're not "most girls" are you, Lacey Teale?'

The boat forced its way across the choppy harbour waters, passed the tiny Fort Denison that had been waiting with its cannon since convict days for Russian warships that never came. Lacey twisted around to see its beacons and single palm tree slide by on their right. Luke put his arm around her.

'I used to take the ferry to Manly when I was about fourteen,' he told her. 'My first girlfriend was a beach lover.'

'But you lived in Campbelltown,' she said. 'That's a long way to come at fourteen for a day at the beach.' She bit her tongue. He'd not told her that. It was information gleaned eagerly from newspapers when she was a teenager herself. But Luke didn't notice.

'I stayed for months at a time with my aunt in Randwick when I started getting serious coaching. To get away for a day at the beach I had to play hooky.'

'It was that rigid?'

'Sure.' He gave a half laugh. 'Tennis has been almost my entire life since Dad put a racquet in my hand when

I was four. Training, coaching, practice, restricted diets—— ' he sighed. 'There wasn't time for much else apart from school.'

'Did you find it boring?' Lacey thought of her own childhood and all those leisurely picnics on the Nepean, of hours of time-wasting books and idle sketches made in the long grass beneath the quince tree.

'Not boring. There were times when I wanted to run away and do what other kids were doing. Surf boarding and loafing around on the beach all weekend, playing pinball machines and riding trail bikes. I did some of them of course, but there was always the regime . . .' he looked faraway. 'But tennis was in my blood. I wanted to be the best, but more than that—I just wanted to play.'

It must have hurt to give it up. She almost said it and steered around the subject.

'Did you know right away? That you wanted to play tennis?'

She saw the interested gaze of an elderly man several rows away. He must have recognised Luke. Looking around she noticed another pair of eyes on him. It must always have been like this for him, only much more intense.

He laughed. 'Damned if I can remember. Tennis was just—there. In my earliest memories. I don't recall any life without it.'

Her heart gave a twist at the poignancy of the words. If he felt like that, why on earth had the scandalmongering of the newspapers made him stop playing? She longed to ask but stayed silent, hoping he might volunteer his reasons. But he didn't.

'How about you, Lacey? Have you always known that you wanted to decorate?' he asked mockingly.

'Well——' she considered it. 'I *did* start moving my bedroom furniture about as soon as I was big enough to push it. And I was *very* fussy about the placement of my dandelion arrangements.'

'Weeds?'

'Yes. I wasn't at all discriminative about what flowers I picked. It became fairly obvious early on that my vocation was *not* for floral art.'

He laughed, pulled her companionably against him and she told him a little about her own untrammelled youth, while the black and glittering heights of the South and Middle Head slipped by and the ferry heaved its way across the strait of open sea to the shelter of the North Head.

It was windy at Manly but it didn't seem to matter. In fact, as Lacey remarked to Luke, it was exactly the right kind of weather.

'Cold, windy nights and hot fish and chips,' she said with relish, rustling the layers of white paper that surrounded her feast. 'Perfect.'

They found shelter of sorts on the southern end of the beach and finished their meal with the remainder of the white wine. The surf roared in, ghostly white tatters of foam in the dark, and the wind blew salt in their face and spray on Lacey's glasses. She couldn't remember a thing she'd eaten in last night's expensive restaurant but she knew she'd never forget this. Afterwards she wasn't entirely sure just what they talked about. For over an hour they sat there idly exchanging nonsense stories about themselves.

'I always wished I had a brother or sister,' she sighed. 'It would have been much more fun setting fire to the old chicken coop with someone else.'

'Lacey Teale—a tomboy?' he quizzed.

'Absolutely. I have my poetic phases but I dressed like a boy, climbed trees and made fires. My parents despaired for my femininity until——' Until I saw you on television one night and remembered I was a girl. How incredible. '—until I just changed, the way girls do.'

'My brother is six years older than me,' Luke put his arm around her, sat close behind her to cut the wind which had whipped her hair into tortuous tangles. 'I used to tag along with him and his cronies—until they scared the life out of me by pretending to be Fisher's Ghost.'

They walked along the beach, taking off their shoes to hang them by the laces around their necks. Luke held her hand.

'Did that prank give you nightmares?' She tried to imagine this large, powerful Luke as a small boy, shrinking with fear beneath the bedclothes.

'For a time. But I grew older and learned there was no such thing as ghosts,' he said with a tinge of self-mockery.

Lacey let the silence stretch between them, aware that though his hand was warm on hers, she had lost him again to that dark moodiness. The sand was cold and damp, the moon white and reluctant beneath a film of cloud. The sea rushed in and backed away in a tireless tumble. She was glad when they walked along the Corso to catch the ferry in the comparative calm of the inner headland.

He drove her home when he discovered that she did not have her car. On the way he was quiet. Lacey gave him directions and he peered up at the apartment block in the quiet Wollstonecraft street as he parked.

'I've enjoyed tonight, Luke,' she said uncertainly at his silent stare.

'Me too.' He got out to open her door, walked with her to the front entrance, then stopped and put his arm around her waist. Lacey raised her face to his, wondering at his intensity.

'Goodnight, Lacey,' he murmured and put his mouth to hers in a brief, gentle salute that should have been the forerunner to that kiss last night, not the follow-up. For a moment she thought he would repeat it, but Luke moved away sharply to his car. The white sports model performed a tight turn and surged away.

Her watch showed her eleven-ten as she opened her door. Four hours ... she flicked her tongue over her lips. They tasted salt. And sweet. But mostly salt.

CHAPTER THREE

SHE hadn't, Lacey thought the next day at her desk, even asked Luke when he wanted her to visit Fremont. It had been all too easy to forget that he was a client.

'It turned out to be mostly business,' she'd lied to Beth to escape the flurry of questions over breakfast. 'He showed me a—a property that he liked which gives me an insight into his tastes.' She felt bad fooling Beth like that. But to tell her what they'd really done, how she really felt, would be to admit someone else to that tenuous magic.

'Where was it—this property?'

'Oh—er—harbourside, you know. Quite big and impressive.' She grinned at her flatmate. As a description of the Opera House it lacked a little perhaps. Beth looked at her thoughtfully.

'Just be careful with him. He's a hunk, I gather, from his photos, but it was only tennis he gave up.'

Lacey smiled as she tackled the pile of waiting paperwork. Beth, two years younger, seemed to believe she needed protection.

Sandra, Logan and Teale's part-time help, arrived. They called her a girl Friday but it was something of a misnomer. Sandra was plump and forty-five and the mother of five children ranging from teens to eight years. Her tales of domestic woe were varied and complex and Lacey and Mike made her arrival the signal to bustle away to the drawing board, phone or out to visit a client. This morning Lacey wriggled out of the tale of teenaged Libby's behavioural problems and busied herself on the phone. Mike was out most of the day. His current project was the layout of a yacht club and he returned from the harbour a trifle windblown, as Lacey finished a return call from Mrs Prentiss who had changed her mind again about her dining-room walls.

'Mike, how would you like to handle Mrs Prentiss' penthouse?'

He ran through his phone messages and grimaced. '*Pink* Mrs Prentiss?'

'We-ll, mostly pink. I did introduce her gently to greys and blues last time. She's definite about colours but otherwise is indecisive. What she needs is a personable young man, trendy but not too far out, with an understanding nature to help her make up her mind.'

'In other words you're palming her off on me.' His tone lacked a little of its usual lightheartedness and Lacey tried to ignore it. During their three-year partnership, they had communicated seriously when necessary, usually over the financial statements, but for the main on an easy, familiar level. She and Mike had the perfect understanding—their tastes and special fields complemented each other. Their sense of humour blended nicely to eliminate many of the strains of a close working relationship and their differences enabled them to handle between them even the most difficult clients. To switch customers was not new. Occasionally a change of approach was exactly what was needed to ensure that the buyer was happy.

'Not if you can't manage it, Mike. But she might relate better to you than to me. As Beth said to me the other night—you *do* have a way with women.' It was a slight re-arrangement of the quote but his disparaging remarks about Beth prompted her to it.

He blinked at her, grey eyes unusually large for a man, and dark lashed. They were an oddity with his tight curled hair and Greco profile.

'You want to offload her I suppose, so that you can concentrate on Harrow's place?'

'That's not fair, Mike.' She flushed.

He ran a hand through his hair. 'No. Sorry.'

'Mike——' Lacey was dismayed at his depressed air. She looked at her watch. Sandra had gone and it was way past closing time. '—let's talk. Take me upstairs to your "little place" and give me a drink.'

'Sure.' It was nothing new. They frequently took their rough sketches and a few samples upstairs and hammered out a problem over a drink in Mike's spacious place over the shop, though she had tried to cut down the frequency since their brief bout of dating.

His flat was an indulgence of Mike's favourite element in interior design. Restraint. If it was possible to indulge in restraint. There was a series of low, low divans with cushions. He had a few sparse pieces of furniture around—tables at Oriental height and an obelisk-shaped display stand of stark glass and ebony bearing a few beautiful ornaments. A weeping fig drooped from a large white tub, a spiky stand of Draecena exploded from another. Uplighters and downlighters, placed unerringly about the room, made the almost all-white interior warm and intimate in spite of the sweeping open spaces. They sat on one of the divans with a drink each and Mike relaxed as they talked.

'I guess I'm going through a crisis,' he admitted at last. 'Soon I'll be thirty.' His lugubrious expression made her laugh.

'Thirty! You're not worried about that surely?'

He looked sheepish.

You are! Mike, for heaven's sake—thirty is young. You've got a fantastic flat, you drive a Chevvy Corvette, have a thriving business—well, almost thriving—do the work you love to do. What more could you have done by thirty?'

'You're right.' He looked around his apartment. 'It's just that sometimes I wonder——'

'What you need is a——' she began thoughtlessly and fell silent.

'Right.'

She bit her lip. 'But not me, Mike. I'm not the one, believe me.'

'Maybe not,' Mike stretched, then folded his arms behind his head. 'But it could be such fun finding out we didn't suit.'

'But you know that we wouldn't, don't you? And why spoil a perfectly good working relationship for a poor gamble?'

'Sensible. So very sensible, Lacey. Have you ever done anything that was a gamble? Ever thrown caution to the devil and rushed in without thinking?'

Her smile disappeared. She had waited today for

Luke to phone, as eager as any teenager with her first love. Too eager to ring him. If he knew when she smiled and removed her glasses on the phone, he would spot eager. Thrown caution to the devil . . . how close was she to doing just that? 'When you come to Fremont, Lacey, you'll be in the devil's court.'

'Yes I have. And gained our Mrs Prentiss as a life-long customer. Had I been cautious I would have put her off at the start by saying I never, but *never* use pink.' She got up to go and he walked downstairs with her.

'Is your car still with mechanic?' the She nodded. 'I'll drive you home on condition that you invite me in for a drink too. I'm not anxious for my own company tonight.'

'Okay. But just a drink. It's our cleaning night tonight and living with Beth that's no joke.'

'When did she say I had a way with women?' he asked as he stopped at the Harbour Bridge tollgate.

'Who—Mrs Prentiss?'

'No. Your messy flatmate.'

'Ah—the night before last I think.'

Lacey smiled at his disguised interest. Mike and Beth? A brief matchmaking urge was squashed as she imagined Beth in his super, uncluttered home. The idea seemed even sillier when she opened the door of her flat to find the living room strewn with Beth's dressmaking things again. Mike raised an expressive eyebrow at the mess and Lacey waved him to the divan.

'Sit down. I'll get you that drink.' He sat next to Beth's brown handbag which was stuffed with trivia and gaping open. As Lacey put a whisky in his hand, Beth herself appeared wearing a half-finished garment that sprouted pins and trailed tacking.

'Oh——' her face dropped when she saw Mike. 'Hello. Are you two going out tonight?' She gave Lacey a strange look. Luke Harrow one night and Mike the next, Lacey could see her thinking. She sounded almost affectedly casual and Lacey remembered now that Beth had always been loath to mention the few dates she and her partner had had outside business. Funny how it hadn't been obvious until now.

'No, of course we're not going out. I wouldn't leave you to do the cleaning alone,' she looked pointedly around. 'Mike drove me home because my car's out of action for another day. That's going to look great when you've finished it, Beth.'

The pale gold tafeta looked good with her friend's colouring. The down-played shade made the most of her perpetual sun tan, brown eyes and the permanent natural colour in her cheeks.

'Like a drink?' Lacey asked her and Beth nodded as she unpinned the side seam and half struggled out of the hazardous garment to reveal her running shorts and t-shirt underneath. She saw Mike giving some thoughtful attention to Beth's better than average legs which were a glorious tan, but he eyed the offcuts and material lying about and said:

'There's more fabric on the floor than in the dress.'

'Well then, perhaps you'd like to cover me a matching chair,' Beth retorted at the critical look in his eye. 'Then when you come I can sit in it and be invisible. And neat,' she added.

There was a knock at the door and Lacey went to answer it, leaving Beth in the clutches of a few wayward pins that refused to dislodge, and Mike just rising to offer his assistance.

'Stand still,' she heard him say, 'It's caught on your shorts.'

She was smiling when she opened the door.

Luke stood there, one arm resting vertically along the door frame, his body on an incline. He straightened and thrust his hands into his pockets.

'I was passing——' he said, eyes on the smile that lingered on her lips, '—and decided to call rather than phone you.'

'Luke.' Pleasure washed over her at the sight of him standing there. The impression of familiarity was strong. As if she'd known him an age. Her fierce, warm welcome translated naturally into words.

'I'm glad you're here,' she said simply, with a brilliant smile and only the sound of Beth's door closing brought her back to reality. 'You can meet my partner,' she added in a bid to come back to earth.

His gaze had already gone past her to Mike who was looking very much at home on the divan, drinking. There was no sign of Beth, apart from her strewn belongings. This was hardly the ideal apartment to show a client, Lacey thought reminding herself again that Luke *was* one. Any trace of style was smothered in the homeliness of Beth's debris and junky pictures and knick-knacks. Her notions of decor were a mix of zany and kitsch. The latest example of both was a large football boot complete with dangling laces. Inside it nestled a leafy pothos in a pot. 'I saw the idea in a magazine' she had told Lacey. Luke's eyes lingered on the unlikely arrangement.

Mike put down his drink and got up, grey eyes speculative as he recognised Luke. Lacey performed the introductions and the men shook hands—Luke with his shuttered expression and Mike with mixed feelings. He was obviously weighing up the other man, no doubt wondering at his appearance at her flat, yet conscious that this was a famous and important client to be treated with deference.

'Luke was passing and called to make arrangements about my visit to Fremont,' she explained to Mike and fetched a drink for Luke. Her hands shook a fraction as she dumped some ice cubes in a glass and poured whisky over them.

'Tomorrow perhaps, Lacey?' Luke said as she handed him the drink. He smiled down into her eyes and she raised a hand to adjust her glasses.

'Well——' Lacey was thinking of her car, out of action for another day.

'Go ahead, Lacey,' Mike said expansively, apparently forgetting her car. 'I can handle any appointments you have.' His tone was familiar, possessive even, and Lacey felt a mild irritation at this subtle, unbased jealousy.

'Are you sure, Mike?'

'Positive.' Mike beamed at her and Luke, for all the world like an owner loaning out his prize possession for a day. If he wanted to give the impression that he had some special relationship with her, he was doing a good job.

'Fine. The most urgent is Mrs Prentiss.' He looked dismayed. Lacey smiled. It served him right.

'Tomorrow then, Lacey.'

'My car is with the mechanic tomorrow——' she began. Luke dismissed any further discussion.

'I'll pick you up at two at your office,' he said to her with a fleeting glance beyond to Mike. 'And bring a change of clothes. We can stay overnight. I'd prefer not to drive back tomorrow evening but I can have you back here early the next morning.' There was a silence and he looked into her eyes, ignoring Mike. 'Well?' he said, challenge in the set of his mouth.

'Yes, that's fine,' she said levelly and went with him to the door. He drew her outside, pushing the door closed.

'Does he live here too?'

'Who, Mike?' Lacey gave a little gasp of laughter. 'No. He has a place above the office. Why?'

'I wondered if you and your partner shared more than office space.'

'I told you—I share with Beth. Mike and I are very good friends as well as partners,' she told him stiffly. 'And it really isn't any of your business, Luke.'

'Do you talk to all your clients like that?'

'Only the nosey ones.'

'I'm not nosey. Just getting the facts straight.'

'Why?'

'I prefer a singles match. Never did go much for mixed doubles.' He ran his eyes over her and Lacey drew herself up.

'I'm not an element in one of your games, Luke.'

'Stupid of me, Lacey,' he said, dead serious. 'I didn't intend to give you the impression that it was a game.'

'That's a very ambiguous statement.'

'Isn't it?'

In their small silence the low conversation of Beth and Mike murmured through the door, followed by a burst of Barbra Streisand. Lacey couldn't drag her eyes from Luke.

'Damn it——' he said and reached out for her. 'I tried to slow it down——' He snatched her against him. His mouth met hers in a brief, turbulent hunger that found an immediate response in Lacey. Her arms wrapped about his back, her lips opened to his. Desire was a heart-racing heat that pressed her closer to him. Luke pulled back before she did, winding down their passion with tender, teasing touches of mouth and tongue. Their breathing slowed.

'Luke, I'm not sure that I can handle this job for you. Maybe Mike had better go down to Fremont tomorrow.'

He released her, said tersely, 'You'll do the job, Lacey—if Logan and Teale want the contract. That's the only way I'll have it.' His eyes met hers once more as he turned into the stairwell. Lacey remained there after he had gone, wondering why the words failed to rankle the way they should. Maybe it was that raw need in his kiss, the memory of that other laughing man who had poured wine in plastic cups and held her hand. And maybe it was that look of vulnerability he'd worn for just a moment.

There was certainly no trace of it the next day when he picked her up. In fact he was taciturn, the lines on his face set deeply, blue eyes shuttered. His replies to her efforts at conversation were sharp and short. She nearly saluted on the last one and gave up. As they passed the University of Sydney Lacey settled into her seat and began to think she had dreamed the strange mental and physical bond that had grown so quickly between them. Her overnight bag was on the back seat and she smiled wryly out the window thinking how she had packed it while her head was full of Luke's possible designs on her. She had almost created a Gothic scenario—the large, brooding, old house waiting for them—his mother mysteriously away for the night— all the staff (if there were any) having their night off— just herself and Luke. . . .

They were passing Warwick Farm Racecourse, outside Liverpool, before he spoke again.

'Your apartment wasn't what I expected.'

'What did you expect?'

'Style—flair—colour   co-ordination.   Exceptional pictures and ornaments.'

She smiled. 'Yes. I had an apartment like that some time ago.' A sigh passed her lips. 'It was a dream. Everything the way I liked it and everything in its place.'

'Your flatmate seems a bit untidy.'

'Yes, she's hopeless.'

Luke glanced at her curiously. 'Then why share with her? I'm sure Logan and Teale must be making enough money for you to manage your rent alone.'

'It does. But I enjoy sharing with Beth.'

'What does she do?'

'She's a secretary. We haven't a lot in common. Except tennis.' At his quick look she added, 'Very bad tennis I'm afraid. We play occasionally. Beth spends most of the summer at Bondi and jogs in the winter. She plays Status Quo while I'm not home. We agree on Barbra Streisand and Air Supply when we're both there.'

'You still haven't explained why you share with her.'

Lacey shuffled in her seat at his tone. 'Do I have to?'

He gave a short laugh that didn't lift the strangely bleak look from his eyes. 'No. Of course not.'

After a pause she said: 'It was nice having a place as near to perfect as I could make it, but it was somehow—empty. Beth is warm and a darned good friend—and I suppose I compromised.'

'More than that. There were a few pictures on your walls that must drive you crazy. And that collection of cutesy ornaments! All junk. A football boot sprouting a pot plant.' He gave a short laugh.

'It's not junk to Beth. And I *am* only sharing after all. Just because I'm a decorator that doesn't give me the right to walk all over her personal tastes.' Her tone was acerbic. First Mike and now Luke with their criticisms of Beth. Or was it a criticism of *her*? Perhaps she gave others the impression that she adhered to the aesthetic values of her profession so rigidly that she couldn't accept any dilution of them.

'I'm glad you didn't send your partner instead.'
Surprise swung her head around to his profile. It was
less touched by time than the full front view of his face.
In profile there was still a hint of the younger man.

'You made it clear what would happen if I did that,
didn't you, Luke? And Logan and Teale want your
contract.'

'Somehow I wasn't sure that that would cut any ice
with you.' He turned and smiled at her and her stomach
flipped a couple of times.

'You're an unusual woman, Lacey.'

Oh good, she thought. Unusual. The description was
oddly unappetising and she gave him a brief, polite
smile, tipped her glasses more firmly on to her nose and
looked out the window at the thinning residential
suburb that was giving way to pastureland and toy-
town dairy herds.

The afternoon sky was cloudy when they reached
Fremont. Luke turned the car into the drive that had, at
one time, swept to the grand old house's door. Now it
limped, apologetic, a bit crumbled at the edges where
weeds overlapped and the garden rambled past the
confines designed for it in bounteous Victorian days.
But there had been slumps, the great depression and
two wars since then and Fremont's fortunes had
declined and risen with a number of owners. The sun
withdrew completely and the house waited for them
against a lowering backdrop of greys and silver-mauve.

It had always fascinated her as a child. The big house
in its sweeping grounds. Of course now she knew that
the funny curved bit like a tower at one side was a
faceted bay wall; that the frosting that fringed the roof
and ran like a panel of petticoat lace right along the
wide, two-sided upstairs verandah and trickled down to
clasp the downstairs pillars, was cast iron lace; the
pleats that divided the upper set of round-headed
windows from the lower, was a moulded string course,
and the carved eyebrows above each window were hood
mouldings. But the house seemed to shrug off
architectural description for Lacey. It could not be
other than 'The Big House' which she had always

craned to see as the family drove past on their way to a picnic spot on the Nepean River. How strange, she thought, suddenly struck by the peculiar pattern. Had 'The Big House' in some small way influenced her to seek a career in decorating so that she could come here now and maybe help give it back a little of its grandeur? Which raised another, similar question.

Had she gazed upon her pictures of Luke all that time ago as a prelude to ... she looked quickly at him as he turned off the ignition. Prelude to what, Lacey? She silently derided her romantic comparison. Will you fall in love with every man whose photograph you ever pinned on your wall in your teens?

'She's a bit of a mess, isn't she?' Luke said, and Lacey stared blindly at the house she'd come to see, not hearing his question while three words of that last one of her own rang in her ears. He got out and opened her door, twitched her bag from the back seat and stood beside her as she gazed up at Fremont. Add another element to the Gothic scenario, she thought. The girl harbours romantic notions about the master of the house while he—he might merely want to claim her as a trophy. When a curtain briefly swished aside in the upstairs bay window, she thought it was an extension of her Gothic meanderings.

'Heavens,' she said brightly—too brightly. 'Your house has such an atmosphere against that dramatic sky that I'm already imagining faces at the upstairs window.'

Luke looked at the window in question without her pointing it out and his face tightened perceptibly.

'It's my mother more than likely,' he said, and Lacey saw the curtains move again as she followed him to the wide stone steps and into the cool gloom of the upper floor overhang. She shivered and thrust her hands into the pockets of her cord jacket. A feeling of depression fell on her.

But it didn't last. Once past the sad, fire-charred entrance hall with its boarded-up door, side panels and ruined oak dado, Lacey was in a state of mixed delight and despair as Luke put down her bag and, seeing her interest, gave her a quick downstairs tour. She found here a magnificent room with its original proportions unmarred—its fireplace and cornices intact—and there a sorry modernised one, its chimney piece replaced with grimly practical panelling over a mock 'fire' of moulded scarlet coals. Luke suggested coffee, but she shook her head and took her notebook from her handbag. He led her through the entire lower floor, then up the broad stairs with their richly carved balustrade. Once or twice she muttered something, jotted down a note and looked up to find Luke smiling at her almost indulgently, his moodiness apparently gone. He carried her bag and left it in a room of modest but good proportions that cried out for something less cumbersome than the full tester bed that crowded it.

'This is your room while you're here,' he said, and she looked again at the bed with its heavy curtains.

'Oh. Good.' She smiled and tried to push away that silly quick vision she'd had of herself—on a bed like this. With him.

'The master bedroom,' he told her as they moved on to a large room at the back of the house. 'Which means of course, mine. The stuff in here is temporary. I'll want you to give me some ideas.'

Lacey stopped in the doorway and looked around at the low, modern furniture that was lost in the room's soaring height and the forward thrust of another bay window. Unusual to put the main bedroom at the back, she thought. Perhaps it had river views.

'You can come in,' Luke said in some amusement when she stayed where she was, 'I never rush the net.'

She forced herself in and made the merest inspection before turning to leave.

'Forming any plans for my room, Lacey?' he enquired, catching her arm.

'Not on one glimpse. It will depend on what you want, Luke.'

Blue eyes shot over her.

'That's easy,' he said softly and drew her close into his arms to match his lips to the shape of protest on hers. But her silent 'no Luke' went up in a puff of smoke and her arms circled his ribs and the tight muscles of his back as if this was perfectly natural. And it never had been, not for her. Not this rightness within mere days of imperfect knowledge of a man. Her body sang in harmony with his—she touched and was touched, kissed and was kissed and it was a blending of passion and tenderness that had not come her way, ever.

He released her and a second later she let him go.

'I thought you said you never rushed the net.' Her voice was shaky.

'That wasn't rushing,' he told her, his eyes smoke blue and warm, so warm. 'If I had rushed you—the door would be locked and you would be there—with me——' he gestured at the bed, eyes never leaving her.

'Luke, this is all too much. I hardly know you——'

He slipped a hand to the back of her neck and his fingers moved in the silky wisps of wayward hair.

'I think I know you, Lacey. It doesn't seem possible that I hardly noticed you that first time. I can't think how I didn't recognise you.'

'Recognise——?' she repeated, and unbidden to her mind came the memory of that photograph of herself, a lanky fourteen displaying her avowal of love. But surely he would never have seen it? His manager no doubt tossed it out with his diminishing bags of fan mail.

'As a woman who would keep me awake at night,' he said.

Relieved, she laughed. 'Come now, Luke. I'm sure other women have kept you awake at night and far more pleasurably than I might have done.'

His fingers bit into her neck. Luke looked seriously at her. 'I've never wasted much sleep over a woman, Lacey. Only once, a long time ago. You've stayed in my mind——' He pulled her close again, hands spread, curved to her shoulders, '—and stayed, and stayed. It's as if——' He stopped, ran a fingertip over the shape of her cheekbone, along her jaw, 'as if I've known you for years, way back when I was young.'

'You're not exactly past your prime now,' she said in breathless light-heartedness. Luke pulled her fiercely to him.

'Don't joke, Lacey. You feel it too, don't you? I saw it on your face when we danced. My God, I went to dinner expecting a discussion with a quiet, hesitant interior decorator and you walked in wearing that green thing and knocked me flat.'

'You hardly spoke to me!' she protested, remembering his aloofness that had made her lose her temper.

'Getting my bearings,' he said in a low voice and put his mouth to hers in an intimate, fleeting caress. 'I didn't intend to be so pushy that night. I don't usually come on so strong. . . .'

'On the first date?' she mocked gently, using his own words.

'I thought I might have scared you off—but I had to see you so I kept it casual——'

'Fish and chips and the Manly ferry,' she mused, smiling. 'You struck just the right note. I *was* a bit shaken by the night before. And guilty too.'

'Guilty?' He said sharply.

'Well——' she hesitated, feeling foolish because here she was doing it again, '—for fraternising with a client.'

'Fraternising!' he laughed. 'I wanted to fraternise with you, Lacey. The funny thing is,' he gave an embarrassed half laugh, 'holding hands on the beach was . . . just right somehow for that night.'

'Yes,' she agreed, thinking of it. 'It was.'

'The day after I tried to tell myself I'd imagined it. But when I saw you again, kissed you, I knew you were going to cause me a lot more sleepless nights.'

'Luke, what are you saying?'

He smiled, blue eyes candid, confused. 'I'm saying that I want you, but you already know that . . . as for love—I'm not sure that I know what that is anymore.' His hands framed her face. 'But you make me feel the way I used to. You remind me of better days when I *did* know.'

Abruptly he bent and kissed her hard, with the fierce hunger of the night before and this time his hands roamed her body, stripping away her last reserve as he searched out the shape of her and turned them from strangers on the brink, to lovers. Almost lovers, Lacey thought as she pushed her hands beneath his shirt and moved her fingertips on the silk-steel of his skin.

Approaching footsteps dragged them apart. They stared at each other, passion still lingering in their eyes. Luke smoothed her ruffled hair, then his own. The clack of shoes in the hall grew louder then stopped.

'Ah, Mrs Simmons,' he said easily as a middle-aged woman appeared in the doorway. 'This is Miss Teale of Logan and Teale interiors. She will be handling the interior design for Fremont. You've arranged some dinner for us around seven have you?'

The woman smiled at Lacey and confirmed the dinner arrangements.

'And how is my mother, Mrs Simmons? Feeling better?'

'Quite a lot better, Mr Harrow. She won't go down for dinner tonight, though. It's probably for the best,' she added with a glance at Lacey.

Luke turned to her. 'My mother's suite need not concern you at this stage. Its decoration will be largely self-contained anyway and can be treated as a separate flat. If you want to go through the rest of the house again—go ahead. The floor plans are on the desk in the study downstairs.'

From his tone you would think they were all business, Lacey thought, dazed by the sudden reappearance of Luke Harrow, client. After a brief struggle, she rose to the occasion.

'Yes, Mr Harrow,' she said with her professional smile and his lips quirked.

'There is a photocopy too, if you want to make any notes directly on to the plans.'

She walked past him. 'No, I won't need to do that just yet. Any ideas I have I will allow to percolate a while before I commit them to paper. I never rush the net.'

Luke gave a crack of laughter that brought a look of surprise to Mrs Simmons' face. Maybe, Lacey thought, he didn't do it too often, even in his home.

She went along the hall with the housekeeper.

'I've put towels in the bathroom for you, Miss Teale, if you want a bath or shower before dinner.'

'Thank you. Is Lu—Mr Harrow's mother sick, Mrs Simmons?'

The woman paused with Lacey at the door of her bedroom. 'I hope you'll find the bed comfortable. Yes, I'm afraid the poor woman doesn't keep the best of health,' she said with a final air. A very firm 'no more questions please' that, Lacey thought, but closed the bedroom door and leaned against it, lost in other questions entirely as she re-played Luke's near declaration in her head. He felt the way she did . . . Lacey let her head drop back against the panelled door and smiled at the elaborate ceiling rose from which the light fitting hung. It was too good to be true.

She went to the French doors and opened them, stepped out on the verandah and walked slowly around from the front of the house to the side. The outbuildings and coach-house nestled in old gardens, surrounded by the crass necessity of scaffolding and piles of building materials apparently intended for repair work. Further on, Lacey could see newly planted gardens and turf and beyond that, the posts and mesh of several completed tennis courts and the mess of more in the making. The grounds were dotted with big old trees—magnolia and cedar and a jacaranda. Beyond them and others were silver glimpses of the river which ran way below the courts complex. As she lingered there, Luke walked out from the house's side door. He had changed into tennis gear. A stray shaft of sunlight from the frowning sky brought a gleam of gold to his dark blond hair. Another, older, man came out of the coach-house. He, too, was in tennis clothes and darted back inside to bring out an armful of racquets. Luke took one, weighed it and slapped his free hand on the strings. It was the old habit of his she had seen so often on television. Between points he always hit the racquet repeatedly against the heel of his hand.

CHAPTER FOUR

THE temptation to go down and watch him play was strong. But Lacey resisted it. She was here on business, she reiterated as her blood sang through her veins and she ignored the tiny niggle of guilt that she had discarded her cardinal rule to remain uninvolved with clients. So she took her notebook and tape and the plans and slowly progressed from room to room again, jotting, measuring and disciplining herself to barricade off the ideas, technicolour visions and immediate emotional responses that, heeded too soon, might set her too rigidly along one path. Wryly, she conceded that she might have done better to obey the same principle where Luke was concerned. But Luke was different. Her dealings with him were not governed by any rules.

Dusk threw shadows into the high-ceilinged rooms and dark purple into the hallways as Lacey finished. She went upstairs and used the echoing tiled bathroom, then changed into a simple cream dress drawn into the waist with a bronze belt. Brushing her hair loose she hesitated over her glasses. Strictly speaking she didn't need them. In the end she wore them. She could always, Lacey thought, take them off.

Descending the grand staircase, she reflected that she should be wearing rustling taffeta and carrying a fan. Her Gothic fancies again, she smiled and headed for the study where she decided to look over the plans until dinner. The door opened under her hand before she heard the male voices.

Luke rose from the desk. He was wearing a track suit over his tennis clothes. Exercise had brought some colour to his cheeks, flopped his hair down over his eyes, but he looked rather grim. The shutters were back. For a moment she doubted that this was the man who had held her, whose eyes had glowed with discovery.

58

'Come in, Lacey. Meet my manager, coach and old friend, Don Marsden.'

It was the man she had seen this afternoon. Don was around the mid-fifties, maybe more, though it was hard to tell. Although he had weathered skin and hard-edged lines around his eyes and mouth, his thickset body was very fit, apart from a slight stomach bulge. He had shrewd, quick-moving brown eyes that flitted from Luke to Lacey in speculation, then remained on her in admiration. Reluctant admiration, she thought.

'Hmmph,' he grunted. 'The only time I had *my* house decorated, I got a pretty young fellow with a wallpaper patterned shirt and limp wrists. You have the luck of the devil, Luke.'

Luke gave a wry smile at that. 'So they say.'

'If you're talking privately——' Lacey began, but Don shook his head.

'Going over old ground, Miss Teale—old ground. Sit down and let's get a look at something new.'

She sat, smiling uncertainly at this cryptic invitation and looked at Luke's face that was tense again. What was the 'old ground' that had banished the laughter from him so absolutely? She nodded at his enquiry about a drink and took a glass of sherry from him as Don quizzed her about her job. He sat in a chair close to Luke's desk, with one elbow on the edge of it, in a pose that looked like second nature to him. Don Marsden looked as if he might have spent a bit of time leaning on pub counters.

'Do many jobs for famous people, do you?' he enquired. 'Celebrities and all?'

'A few.' The shrewd eyes fixed on her. Lacey wondered where this line of conversation was heading. It didn't seem entirely idle to her.

'Who, for instance?' he prompted. 'Any television folks—politicians?'

Lacey smiled. 'If you want to know whether I'm a blabbermouth, Mr Marsden, the answer is no.'

The man raised his brows and glanced at Luke. 'Sassy, isn't she? What about all this name-dropping you folks do, to get more orders? You can't tell me you won't go around boasting that you decorated Luke Harrow's house for him.'

'I can and will tell you exactly that, Mr Marsden. Luke hasn't asked me to take the official secrets oath but if he does I certainly won't be "boasting" as you call it.'

'Go on—you'll have the press after you and what woman could resist telling them any little tit-bits about his private life that she might have come across while she was fixing up his curtains?'

'This woman could,' she said firmly, wondering what 'tit-bits' Don had in mind. 'Our clients enjoy confidentiality.'

'And if you can't use the job for advertising, what do you get out of it?' he cut in.

'Why, Mr Marsden, didn't you know? I'll get a whopping great cheque out of it.'

Luke laughed, tilting back his head. Don's eyes narrowed on him.

'What's so funny?'

'Just a private joke, Don.' Don frowned even harder and Luke smiled at Lacey, his tension gone. She smiled back, delighted that it was she who had made the change in him, and shook her head as he came over to her with the sherry decanter.

'Sorry about the grilling, Lacey. Don is inclined to be—protective.' He stood there a moment studying the attractive picture she made. 'I like you with your hair down,' he murmured with a wicked, heated look that she knew was designed to discomfort her.

'Yours is nice too,' she said composedly and he laughed, ran a hand through the damp, fair thatch falling over his forehead.

'Have you signed a contract yet?' Don interposed.

'Not yet. Lacey will submit her plans and costs and then we'll sign one.'

'Of course,' she put in, heart sinking at the thought, 'should Luke dislike my designs and ideas he'll no doubt get alternative quotes.'

Don Marsden stood up and drained the last of the beer from his glass. Dryly he said: 'Somehow I don't think he's going to dislike your—designs and ideas—do you, Miss Teale?'

Her cheeks flamed. His meaning was explicit. As if she was some cheap little sexpot, using her feminine wiles to get a contract.

'A word with you, Don,' Luke bit out and followed the older man outside. She heard their voices interlocking in argument, then a surprised silence followed by a few low words. Luke was back seconds later.

'My apologies. Don has known me since I was a kid and he oversteps the mark sometimes in his efforts to protect my interests.'

'Is it what *you* think, Luke?' she asked, mortified that she hadn't seen the danger of her responses being misinterpreted.

Laughing, he came over to her and pulled her from her chair. The last drops of sherry spilt from her glass as she clutched it against Luke's chest.

'Do I think you've lured me into giving you the job?' His hand played up the long, tense curve of her spine, thrust into her hair. 'You've lured me all right, Lacey, love. But the job will go to you because you're a talented, capable woman. Not because I fancy you.'

The words didn't reassure her as they might. It was that word. Fancy. But he touched his mouth to hers in a kiss so light that she might have imagined it and his restraint made her almost weak with desire. He put her aside and smiled and Lacey knew that he had done it deliberately. Such expertise, she thought uncomfortably. But only for a second.

'Wait for me in the small dining room. I'll shower and be back in ten minutes.'

And he was, looking powerful and touchable in a thin polo-necked sweater over pale grey trousers. Lacey sat opposite him at the table and tried to look as if business was on her mind when Mrs Simmons came in with a casserole.

'It's very good,' she told Luke, upon tasting it.

'I wish it was fish and chips in paper.'

'With wine in plastic cups and a stiff breeze blowing.'

'And a two-way ferry ride——'

'With your fans ready to pounce.'

'Fans?'

'Didn't you notice? There were two Harrow fans on board just waiting their chance to ask for an autograph. I was all ready to swear you were plain Ralph Brown to put them off the scent.'

He looked injured. 'Ralph I can take . . . but *plain*?'

'Conceited!'

His smile reached every part of his face making him a dozen times more attractive than he'd ever been in his young, untried handsomeness. 'A very dangerous animal.' Beth's words sounded a warning at the sudden hectic pace of her heartbeat. He took her hand and she looked down at their entwined fingers, conscious of a twinge of uneasiness from that wary part of her. The part that had never rushed in and thrown caution to the devil. But it looked so right—her hand in his. It *felt* so right.

They schooled their faces for Mrs Simmons between courses. The dessert was delicious, their cross-table banter more so.

'We'll have coffee in the sitting room, Mrs Simmons,' Luke said and they strolled in silence to the room that was furnished with some rather chintzy two-seaters and single chairs and small, polished walnut tables. Luke went to the tape deck concealed behind a sliding cabinet door and put on some music.

'You said you liked Air Supply,' he said, and she raised her brows.

'You don't miss anything, do you?'

'I have been.'

'Have been what?'

'Missing things. Missing you.'

'But you only met me four days ago.'

'There you are. I had all the days before those to miss you.'

There was a lump in her throat. Did he mean that? It was crazy, fantastic. Too good to be true. The song lyrics filled the pause . . . '—you're every woman in the world to me——'

They drank coffee, listened to the tape until it stopped with a loud click. Luke got up and reversed the cassette. She watched him. Even in the sweater, his left arm development was noticeably more than his right. Luke obviously stayed in training and not just for his work as a coach.

'Luke, will you ever play in competition again?'

'I'm too old,' he said lightly. Lacey looked closely at him. He answered as if he was asked that often. His hand was tense on the arm of his chair.

'Not necessarily. Look at Rosewall. And Connors made a comeback to win Wimbledon in his thirties.'

He shook his head. 'He hadn't been off the circuit for ten years.'

'Why have you?' she asked bluntly. Luke's left hand gripped the chintzy armchair.

'Look, Lacey——' he began roughly then looked at her. 'Let's say, I became disillusioned after my father's death. You know about that?'

'A bit.'

'It wasn't exactly the way it seemed——' he appeared to hesitate over telling her more. 'Anyway I wanted out. I've thought about going back a few times, but——' he shrugged and gave a careless grin. 'I'm satisfied with things the way they are.'

The chintz was crumpled beneath his fingers. She wondered just what he was crushing in that powerful left hand.

'I don't believe you,' she said before she thought. Luke's face darkened.

'You know nothing about it, Lacey. I wanted to be the best and for a while—I was. That's it.'

'You said you wanted something more than to be the best. Just—to play.'

'I do play,' he said on a harsh note. 'Every bloody day. But let me tell you, Lacey, it would have to be a matter of life or death before I played in public again.'

She felt like saying it might already be a matter of *life*. He was only half living she suspected, without the career that had taken all his youth. Again she'd lost him to those old ghosts and she wished in a way she'd not given in to her urge to know about him. His eyes were faraway, even hurt. Ten years after, and he couldn't go back. Luke Harrow was afraid.

'Well,' she said cheerfully, 'perhaps when you get our whopping great bill, you'll be driven to the veteran's circuit to pay it.'

That brought him round. 'Veterans?' he said in astonishment.

Lacey opened her eyes wide. 'Good lord, yes. You're too decrepit for anything else. One has only to *look* at you!'

A slow smile dislodged the past from his eyes. 'Bitch,' he murmured.

'Shabby, bygone glamour——' she went on, teasing, trying to erase the last remnant of tension from him with words. 'You'd be the idol of the blue-rinse set. . . .'

The chintz was safe. Luke got up and advanced on her.

'No decorator says that to me and gets away with it. In fact, Lacey Teale——' he paused, leaned over her, a hand on each chair arm.

'Oh, you're *not* going to say "it's curtains for you" are you?' she laughed up at him, 'I've been hearing that since I was eighteen.'

'Then I'll have to think of something new, won't I?' he said softly and went back to his chair when Mrs Simmons came in to collect the coffee cups. After she'd gone they talked of books and art and his early travels as a country boy player in the sophistication of international tennis.

'The presentations were the worst,' he told her. 'All that bowing in Tokyo and the kissing in France.'

'Hmm, tough for a simple country boy. But I'll bet you soon got the hang of it. The bowing. And the kissing.'

He grinned. 'I was a fast learner.'

'And now?'

'Times have changed,' he grinned. 'Women don't fall into my arms anymore. I have to use a little persuasion nowadays.'

'Tch, tch, what a bore for you.'

'No—I find it fascinating,' he said with a look that could have been interpreted a dozen ways. As if she might be just another fascinating challenge, for one. On the other hand he might mean it quite literally. Lacey chided herself. She was doing what Mike had accused her of. Hiding. Fending off several persuasive men over the past years had made her too cautious by far. At twenty-five she was soon going to have to commit herself and stop this back and forth game she played internally. When he stood up at last, Luke was relaxed and smiling.

'Walk with me, Lacey?' He held out his hand and she took it without question.

They went across the drive, guided by the soft light of the coach lamps set at its side, until they stepped into the dim privacy of shadow on the lawn. Her hand felt right in his. The evening was cool, moonless. A moody night.

'This tree will be beautiful when it flowers,' she looked up at the almost bare branches of the jacaranda just visible against the clouded night sky. In spring the old tree would be a mass of purple set at a regal distance from the pale, warm stone of the house. The wind stirred the scant remaining leaves and one dropped to the ground near them. Lacey bent to pick it up and as she held it, a shower of its tiny leaflets fell at her feet. She twirled the dried stem and its few clinging ellipses and let it go. When she would have walked on, Luke caught her by the wrist and for the space of a sigh they stood there, arms at full stretch.

'Lacey——' he bent his arm, drew it to his side and her with it. 'There are things—other things I should tell you,' he murmured and his breath touched warm on her forehead. 'There are things I want to know about you. . . .' His arms went around her and the darkness pressed close. The tree's branches moved again and the breeze sent more leaves to the ground and brought with it the distant rumble of thunder. 'But I don't think I can wait,' the words whispered against her mouth, his breath expelled in a rush and he pressed a kiss to her jaw beneath her ear, then another and another along her neck to her shoulder until she said his name on a wave of longing.

He kissed her and she opened her mouth and kissed him in return, pushed her hands beneath his sweater to curve them about his sides. Luke moved her until she leaned against the jacaranda and his hands framed her face, tilted it for another kiss that scorched its way through to even that small remaining wary part of her. Down, his hands slipped silkily, down the long line of her neck, his thumbs circling in the hollowing of her throat—along her shoulders, over her breasts and down to her hips. And back again. This time to ease away the cross-over bodice, to dip beneath to the bare upper slopes and the lace-covered lower fullness of her breasts. And then to reach beneath this last barrier to caress and tease until her fingers dug into his back. Bending to her breast, he drew the nipple into his mouth and any last vestiges of Lacey's caution vanished in a silver burst of sensation. She rumpled his sweater up around his ribs, reached for his belt buckle and unfastened it. The time for commitment had arrived. Luke made a low sound, half-laugh, half-moan, then gripped her wrists.

'I want to make love to you, Lacey—slowly——' he leaned forward and pressed his open mouth to hers. 'If I come to your room, will you let me stay?'

'Yes,' she said as she knew she would have to say to Luke sooner or later. 'Yes—I want you, Luke.' Her laugh was low, excited and faintly embarrassed as he restored her dress to order. With his arm around her waist they went back to the house, blinking a little at the soft coach lights. A few drops of rain fell as they reached the cover of the house.

'Ten minutes,' he whispered wickedly in her ear. 'To keep up appearances for Mrs Simmons.'

She gave a foolish, loving laugh and almost ran up the staircase where she had imagined her forlorn ghosts of another time. Now she was not concerned with yesterday, but with the present, and Luke. Even so when a white shape materialised out of the gloom, she gasped. Her heart, already racing, picked up tempo.

'Who is it?' she said stupidly and a light came on. A woman stood there, hand on the switch.

'I'm sorry if I alarmed you,' she said with a smile. 'I'm Paula Harrow.'

'Oh,' Lacey smiled in relief and with a certain amount of uneasiness. There was something offputting about meeting the mother of the man you were about to make love with, she thought, and a flush suffused her face.

'I'm Lacey Teale from Logan and Teale Interiors. You've been ill I hear. Are you all right now?'

Paula Harrow was wearing a frilled nightgown and a matching dressing gown in cream. Lacey remembered that wisp of white on the stairs earlier. Could that have been Mrs Harrow?

'Fine, thank you. I'm looking forward to talking with you about the decoration for my rooms, but in the meantime I——' she paused, frowning. 'I felt I should speak to you. To warn you.' Again that far-off rumble of thunder.

'Warn me?' A prickle of fear crept up Lacey's spine. The old house creaked a few times, the gloom pressed in around the pathetically pale wall light near them. Gothic fancies again, she thought on a sudden wild note. The woman probably wanted to warn her that her bedroom window sometimes jammed, or the doorknob was loose. . . .

'About Luke.' His mother looked at her keenly. 'He has a reputation for chasing girls——'

'Oh.' Lacey said lamely. This had nothing to do with her. She was different from any of Luke's 'girls'.

'I suppose it seems strange. Me, of all people saying this to you,' Paula Harrow said. Her hand moved to her hair, patting it unnecessarily into place with small, nervous movements. 'But I suppose in a way I feel a certain responsibility. You're a very attractive girl, Miss Teale. Just remember that Luke can wrap women around his little finger.' She looked closely at Lacey and added shrewdly, 'They all think they're the only one while he wants them.'

Cold was seeping through Lacey. The only one? She

knew she was not the only one. But different. She was different from the others. 'You're not "most girls" are you, Lacey Teale——?'

'Mrs Harrow——'

'I'm afraid he tells them whatever is necessary to get what he wants. He always has. Luke has a romantic way with words—I'm sure you know what I mean.'

'I had all the days before . . . to miss you——' The long hall was freezing. Lacey shivered.

'Mrs Harrow, I don't think you need to tell me this,' she said desperately, wishing she'd never heard a word of it.

'Maybe not.' Paula Harrow smiled and lightly touched Lacey's arm. 'I suppose I'm worrying unduly. You look a sensible girl. But Luke——' she shook her head. 'He's charming and sweet but not a very moral man. Married or single, he takes what he wants. Where women are concerned he's a—a devil.'

Something odd, almost frightening appeared in her eyes, but it was a trick of the light. Luke's mother was smiling. 'It all sounds very melodramatic I daresay, especially in this old house. But as you are likely to be staying here now and then while the place is decorated, I thought it worth a word of warning. Perhaps I'll see you at breakfast? Goodnight, Miss Teale. Sleep well.'

Sleep well. She meant it, Lacey thought, as she closed her bedroom door. But it might as well have been a mockery. Sleep well. When she had planned to spend the night in Luke's arms—confident that the strange bond they had built in so short a time was real. She clasped her hands, walked around the room, touched the curtains that hung from the bed's tester. Maybe his mother was wrong. Her hand moved up and down on the faded fabric. Maybe all those moving, beautiful things Luke had said were straight from the heart. '—holding hands was . . . just right . . . as for love, I'm not sure that I know what that is anymore . . .' words that had turned her resistant heart in her chest. Words that had made her want to show him that his capacity to love had not died . . . she snatched her hand from the bed curtains and paced around again. The dressing-table mirror showed her framed glimpses of herself as she passed back and forth, and finally she stopped to brush a few jacaranda leaflets from her hair—remnants of a love scene that might have been played out there many times before. If his mother was right, then all his moving phrases might have been designed to make her feel just the way she had when she'd run up the stairs. And how could she dismiss what Paula Harrow had said? A mother wasn't likely to say such harsh things about a son like Luke unless it was true.

Of course, she thought, it was odd that his mother should warn her at all ... the curtains swelled at the open windows. Lacey went to close them. The smell of rain and earth was a cool blast in her face.

There was a gentle tap. Then another. She spun and stared at the panelled door, then the curtained bed. Even doubting, she could have her night with Luke. Slowly she went to the door and opened it. Her heart gave a massive jolt at the sight of him standing there, eyes alight with promise and warmth. That wasn't an act, she thought. Surely not. If his mother was wrong then Luke would not object to waiting a while for this night and if she was right. ... Luke searched her face and tensed.

'Luke—I'm sorry. I've changed my mind——'

She might have done better to plead a headache—that grand, old, classic excuse she thought bitterly the next day, on her way back to the city in the Alfa. Her flat honesty had sparked off a scene she would not soon forget. And the fact that it had been conducted in a harsh undertone had done nothing to lessen its ghastliness.

Luke had pushed his way inside and shut the door noiselessly, not for the clandestine reasons he had hoped, but the better to turn his soft fury on her.

'Changed your mind?' he hissed between gritted teeth, 'Not fifteen minutes ago you were undressing me. Explain—please, what happened between those earthy responses outside and this—this frigid reception.'

If anything confirmed her fears it was this angry, thwarted reaction. Luke was to be denied his reward and he was reacting accordingly. All those loving words had gone with rejection. Humiliation sparked into a dull, aching anger. If only he had pursued her openly—followed up that first declaration of intent with an honest attempt to get her into his bed. She could accept that—even laugh about it. But Luke had guessed that nothing short of her emotional involvement would achieve what he wanted and he'd set out to make her fall for him. The one time she allowed herself to remove her usual restraints had to be with a man who would probably notch up the experience on the handle of his tennis racquet. She could tell him that she had thought she was different from all the others. But if he knew that, he would guess just how vulnerable she remained. And if he tried his sweet persuasion on her again—in here—'You're very attractive, Luke. And I suppose I was impressed by the legend——' It sounded false, frivolous. She gave an embarrassed half-smile and pushed her glasses firmly on, '—and you make it so darned hard for a girl to say no.'

'Don't give me that,' he bit out and grabbed her by the shoulders. 'We had something going. *Have* something going—and that rubbish about legends doesn't wash. You wanted me honestly, openly and didn't trouble to hide it. For God's sake, Lacey, I'm not a boy wet behind the ears. Don't you think I know when a woman feels more than just fascination for my image?'

'I know you're not wet behind the ears, Luke. That's just the point isn't it? You've honed your system to perfection on a long line of other women.'

He shook her so that her glasses jumped up and down on her nose and her hair flopped over her forehead.

'I'm no monk, Lacey. I never claimed to be. Right at the start I told you that I wanted you and you didn't back off then.'

'And I told *you* that I wouldn't be one of your trophies.' She flung at him, her tone as angrily low as his. Lacey was angry at him for being the way he was, angry that his mother had to tell her that her own

almost smothered wariness about Luke had been
justified. Knowing it, she had to refuse him. But had
she not known, she could even now be with him in the
old-fashioned bed with its curtains. . . .

'You, one of *my* trophies! That's a laugh. The way
you behaved tonight, I'm beginning to think you're one
of the groupies who have a hit list of celebrities to work
their way through,' he dragged her closer at her
outraged gasp. 'But you're something new, Lacey—
most of them usually follow through when they've put
the goods on the line.'

She slapped him then, an unsatisfactory hit impeded
by her lack of elbow room, but one that made his eyes
blaze.

'You left it a little late to change your mind,' he said,
and she tried to pull away at the silky, dangerous tone.
'In fact, *too* late.' He pushed her backwards so that she
fell on the bed, one foot catching at the curtains so that
they swished on their wooden rings. She had no sooner
levered herself upright on her elbows than Luke was
there, his hands on her shoulders forcing her down, his
body overlapping hers. 'You said you wanted me,
Lacey,' he reminded her. 'And here I am.'

He kissed her hard, holding her down when she
struggled.

'Lacey——' he growled, raising his head just inches
above hers. The savage light had dimmed in his eyes.
'You said—I thought—dammit.' She held her breath,
sensing the change in him even before his hands
softened on her.

'Why, Lacey love?' he whispered. 'I thought we'd
reached some kind of understanding. Is it too soon after
all?' He dropped quick, melting kisses on her face
between the words. Here it is, she thought, wanting to
give way to the magic but unwillingly recognising it for
the persuasion she feared. Luke would not lose his
reward without using every weapon at his disposal.

'Are you worried that we might not make it together?
Don't be. It will be good for us, Lacey. I know. . . .' His
hands twined in her hair, his lips found the hollow of
her neck and she closed her eyes as his touch began to

turn aside caution. 'Make it together'—how she wanted to.

'Forgive me for saying those stupid things...' he gave a rueful laugh. 'My temper isn't good at any time and I—I want you so much——' He dropped his head to her breast and it would have been so easy to put her arms around him and forget anything but the present.

'Luke—really, I'm sorry. I meant what I said. I've had second thoughts and—don't want to sleep with you. Not just——' 'Not just yet' she was going to say. Even now she had to leave the door open, just in case.

But Luke sat up, his face tight with anger. Leaning over her he said jerkily, 'Second thoughts! What's the matter, Lacey? Have you just remembered more details of my scandalous past—how all that high living and jet-setting made such a negligent bastard of me that I killed my own father? Is that it Lacey—you don't find you can bring yourself to sleep with a man like me?'

He thrust himself from the bed. 'It's a pity you didn't have second thoughts sooner, Lacey. Before you let me believe——' he chopped the words off and left her, just as she'd seen in that one quick, mental picture. Her on the bed with the cushions and the curtains. But alone.

'So what colour scheme of yours put him in such a cranky mood?' Don Marsden enquired with a long look at her faraway face. The Alfa purred along under his guidance.

'I don't know what you mean,' she said a little stiffly.

'Sure you do. Last night he chewed my ears off for daring to suggest his lovely little decorator was stringing him along, and this morning he offloads you on to me, instead of taking the cosy drive to town with you himself.'

Chewed his ears off? Lacey recalled Don's insinuations and the short, sharp exchange that followed it in the hall. Why would Luke bother to defend her?

'What happened—did you lock him out?' The blunt assumption, an astute one at that, took her breath away. A slow colour waved up over her face.

'Yeah—that's what I thought,' Don nodded. 'Look,

Miss Teale, I'm a man who says what he thinks. I call a spade a spade——'

'Yes. I *had* noticed that Mr Marsden.'

'—and believe me, I didn't set out to offend you. But Luke is like a son to me. Always was, even when his father was alive—but that's old ground. If I was a bit rough on you last night, I beg your pardon.' He glanced at her again and this time there was a pleating of anxiety on his forehead that made him look older than she had thought. 'Most humbly,' he added, and it was such a contrast to his former abrasiveness that she smiled.

'All right, Mr Marsden. Apology accepted.'

'It's like this you see—the others—the girls he's had, lookers all of them but much of a muchness. But you— now here I thought, is one who is different.'

So did I. Lacey closed her eyes momentarily. So did I. 'Really? In what way?'

'He seemed to have a—special sort of respect for you.' Don shrugged. 'That's the best way I can describe it, I suppose. He's normally so damned cool where women are concerned that I pricked up my ears when he mentioned you.'

'And that accounts for your interrogation last night? What did you think I would do to him, Mr Marsden?' she asked with heavy irony. She was the one with a heavy great stone in her chest. There was a long silence.

'There's a certain kind of woman could destroy Luke,' he said and she felt that shiver up her spine again at the melodramatic words. 'I've picked up the pieces once and I don't want to have to do it again.'

What woman had shattered Luke Harrow, she wondered. Luke himself had mentioned a woman—one other who had kept him awake at night. But that had been lines from his playboy script. Hadn't it?

'You needn't worry about me, Mr Marsden.'

'You're going to be around quite a bit.' Don said pointedly. 'He stills wants you to do the decorating for him.'

'Yes.' She frowned. That was surprising. This morning she'd expected him to tell her not to bother turning in any designs. Instead, he had waved her to a chair at the breakfast table, put aside his newspaper and given her a run-down of his expectations for the house. It was by far the most concrete discussion they'd had— uncluttered as it was by the innuendo of the others.

'Concentrate first on the living and dining rooms and the main guest suite,' he'd said. 'Give me your ideas on those as soon as you can. If I like them, I'll want them implemented and the rooms ready by late September. My brother will be arriving from England to stay for some time. My brother—and his wife.' The deadline was well ahead of the one he'd originally stated but she forbore to protest. It was a miracle that Logan and Teale were to get the work at all after last night. A miracle and maybe one big headache.

'You'll be staying over the odd night I suppose if he's to have the rooms ready for Gerry and Ruth.'

'Possibly.'

Don muttered something about Luke being a 'bloody fool' and 'wearing a hair shirt' and Lacey couldn't make out if it was inspired by Luke's unchanged decision to have her work for him or by the visit of his brother and sister-in-law. But the time he dropped her off at the office she realised that there was a likeable man beneath the brutally frank exterior, likeable so long as you meant no harm to Luke Harrow.

She was thoughtful as she walked into the converted Paddington terrace houses that were labelled in brass, *Logan & Teale Interiors*. Two people who loved Luke and two entirely different views. His mother warned her lest she become his victim and his manager warned her lest she victimise him. At least that was how it had sounded. There was something odd—very odd—about it all. With her hand on the brass doorknob, she paused and a series of impressions built a collage in her mind— ragged glimpses of a face at the window, a rustle on the stairs, an unveiling of something out of place in Mrs Harrow's gentle, suffering eyes. Luke's face, angry and hurt beyond mere sexual frustration with one of his women. Don Marsden's chilling '—a certain kind of woman could destroy Luke.'

Two starlings swooped overhead. Lacey turned the doorknob. Heavens, she was behaving like the heroine in a Gothic romance again. All imaginings and forebodings.

CHAPTER FIVE

FORTUNATELY, Mike had only the briefest opportunity to quiz her on the professional details of her night at Fremont before Sandra came and scattered them with her opening news of rebellious Libby. But Sandra was gone again at four and Lacey found herself flagging and under scrutiny from Mike. Uneasily, she had reviewed last night's sequences and this morning's and had the feeling that she had missed something somewhere. Time and time during the day she had come back to it, worrying it.

'How about a meeting of the minds later, Lacey,' Mike said. 'I need to give you an update on the Prentiss saga and there are one or two things I'd like to throw in about the Harrow job.'

'Sure.'

'Stay for a steak? I can toss a salad and you can toss around anything that's on your mind.' He gave her a smile and a burst of concern from those grey eyes. It must be showing, she realised, and strengthened her camouflage.

'Why not? I'd better ring Beth first.'

Her flatmate was intrigued to hear about her night at Fremont but her voice lost some warmth when Lacey told her she might stay for dinner with Mike.

'Oh. Fine,' she said.

'It's business.'

'Why should I want to know if its business?' Beth demanded, 'You're both over eighteen. Anyway, I'll be out. I have a date with Brett tonight.'

'It's okay with Beth,' Lacey told her partner. 'She's going out with a man she works with tonight.'

'Uh-huh.'

She was mulling over some rough drawings for Luke when Mike went upstairs. 'Bring the Fremont plans when you come, Lacey.'

'I'll be up in about ten minutes,' she told him and went to lock the front door. A few minutes later she went back to it when someone knocked. Darn it, she thought tiredly. She flung open the door and her mind swept clean. Luke was there. He was wearing business clothes and a frown that influenced every line on his face. Forbidding, unfriendly, formidable was how he looked. A man to keep away from. Lacey wanted nothing more than to put her arms around him.

'I phoned you at home. Your friend said you were working late.' He walked in, looking about at the old interior that Mike had transformed with floating ceilings and stark steel and glass fittings. Hands shoved in pockets, he turned to face her, his eyes moving broodingly over her neat pinned-back hair and the knitted suit in which she had left his house that morning.

'Last night, Lacey——' he began harshly and she coloured.

'Maybe we should forget last night,' her voice was low and in confusion she moved towards his drawings and the sanity of business matters. Luke's fingers closed about her arm, halted her, inched her back to him.

'I don't want to forget it,' he snapped. 'I want to know why it happened—or why it didn't happen maybe I should say.'

'Luke, I told you—I came to my senses that's all, after a little temporary madness.' If only she could give him the truth. But she wasn't sure enough for that. He turned her all the way around and took her shoulders. A lump rose in her throat and she gabbled to dislodge it. 'I knew from the start about your reputation and the breathing space merely allowed me to remember that. It's old fashioned I suppose, but I'm just not the kind to go to bed for a few thrills. . . .'

His eyes were blue—deep, heart-wrenching blue, and they looked intensely into hers. From her shoulders his hands slid down over her arms to take her hands and lose them in his. It reminded her of walking hand in hand on the beach, the wind blowing salt. . . .

'Lacey—don't you think I *know* that?'

It was barely above a whisper, but the words shouted at her. He meant it. There was no mistaking his sincerity. She could *feel* the way he felt and her knees wobbled at the sensation. Maybe her instincts had been right all along. To Luke she *was* the one girl who was different.

'Have dinner with me, Lacey, and we'll talk,' he urged, clasping her hands tightly. 'Anywhere you like, and I won't even try to change your mind again. . . .' He put his mouth to hers, moved it in a charged caress. 'Well, perhaps just a little persuasion——'

'Luke——' she breathed, and a 'yes' hovered on her tongue, unsaid a moment too long.

Mike called as he came down the stairs.

'Are you ready partner? I'm just about to have a shower. Come on up and scrub my back then we'll nip into my bedroom for the Charge of the Light——' His thumping steps sounded on the treads; as he turned from the last step and stopped, Lacey pulled her hands from Luke's. Incredibly, she'd forgotten all about Mike.

'Ah—Mr Harrow.' Mike came over and put a hand on Lacey's shoulder. The gesture said 'mine' loud and clear and she was irritated by it. He held out his right hand to Luke. 'Lacy hasn't been able to stop talking about Fremont. Come and have a look at the rough sketches she'd done for you. . . .' He led the way, talking genially all the time, cementing himself and Lacey as a pair with every word. 'In fact, when we've had dinner upstairs—I have an apartment over the premises—we'll probably have a bit of a session about it to iron out any problems.' He managed to make it sound as if it was only one of the things they had in mind after dinner. Lacey was exasperated. A few dates with Mike and he had developed this possessiveness that sprang more from aimlessness than anything else. Luke shuffled the drawings with a tight-lipped expression.

'They're fine. Ring me when you've got some colours sorted out and I'll have a look at them again.'

Mike excused himself. 'Will you be long, Lacey?' he said warmly and she shook her head. His footsteps bumped away upstairs and there was silence.

Luke went to the front door and she followed him.

'Why didn't you just say you were committed elsewhere?' he said as he opened the door with a savage forehand backsweep.

'You said you felt guilty—was that what dampened your enthusiasm? You suddenly remembered poor, trusting old Mike when you dashed upstairs to wait for me, did you?'

Her mouth opened and shut. She *had* felt guilty, but for letting herself become involved with a client.

'No, Luke, it wasn't like that——'

'My God—and I thought you were different.' He gave a rough laugh and went, leaving the words she'd so wanted to hear hanging ironically in the air.

'Very cosy little scene,' Mike remarked when she climbed his white-carpeted stairs.

'Well, you certainly put a stop to that,' she snapped. Mike gave a low whistle.

'So—the pin-up boy hasn't lost his fascination.' His full mouth twisted. 'I had a feeling all along that——'

'Oh shut up, Mike.'

It was so unexpected from Lacey that he was floored.

'I came up to discuss two jobs with you, so let's get down to it shall we? Forget the steak for me. I'm not hungry.'

She laid out the plans for Fremont and forced herself along its corridors unemotionally. In the end she chided Mike for his possessiveness, he apologised and so did she, for snapping at him. He persuaded her to eat one of his steaks after all, and she even laughed a little at his efforts to cheer her up.

'Let me run you home. When do you pick up your car?'

'Tomorrow morning. I'll get Beth to drop me off at the garage on her way to her Saturday shopping spree.'

'Who's the fellow she's seeing?' Mike enquired casually.

'Brett something. Nice guy—he has one of those all-year-round tans like Beth. He's a surf enthusiast, too.'

'Ah—a beach boy. All muscles and white hair?'

She smiled at his tone. Nothing between the ears, he

meant. 'Certainly not short on muscles. He's an Economics Graduate I believe.'

'Uh-huh.'

Luke was on her mind. Twice she picked up the phone to call him and twice put it down again. And she answered incoming calls more promptly than usual. But he didn't ring. Every day, driving to and from work, she passed within a stone's throw of the NSW Lawn Tennis Association courts—White City—where Luke had won and lost so many years ago. Mostly won. And it reminded her of that glimpse of fear in him, and longing. Lacey began to realise that she knew nothing about the complex Luke Harrow. Nothing.

The rough drawings for Fremont began to overlap into Lacey's free time. Most nights she took them home and chewed her pencil over them until they began to take shape. Each day she whizzed around town, checking her sources of supply, gathering samples for the visual presentation she would have to make to Luke. On the weekend she took a break and went home to visit her parents near Camden, just a half hour or less from Fremont itself.

It was the usual, crazy experience. Her parents were always on their way somewhere, taking evening classes in things like Bonsai and Saw Sharpening, or the house was full of visitors. Her father ran a hardware store and her mother a variety of committees, and her father. All in the most amiable way.

'Decorating *whose* house?' her mother exclaimed when she told her about the Harrow job.

'You mean "The Big House"?' Graham Teale said. 'Well, well fancy Luke Harrow buying that. Just about marries off your two major obsessions, doesn't it, love?'

'What do you mean, Dad?'

He gave her a sly grin. 'The Big House and Luke Harrow. I seem to remember you were mad about them both when you were a kid.'

He went off to his Saturday golf and when her mother had gone to a Bowls Club committee meeting, Lacey made her way to the spare room and found the trunk that stored her earliest memories of Luke. It was the wierdest sensation to unroll that poster—the one that had lurked behind her clothes. The camera had caught him at three-quarter angle, knees bent and feet wide apart in preparation for a groundstroke, the powerful more muscled left arm already well back with the racquet, the right flung forward in graceful counterbalance. She took out the scrapbook in which she had pasted every little clipping about Luke.

Victory again for our Luke the headlines ran in the early days ... *Italians love Luke ... Attaboy Luke ...* golden pictures accompanied these. Luke downing a beer after a tournament—holding a trophy aloft— smiling with an arm around the opponent who defeated him. She turned the pages. The smiling boy began to fade.

'*Wimbledon champ on charge?* Luke Harrow, current Wimbledon champion could be charged with negligence following the death of his father, Gerard Lucas Harrow. A car driven by the tennis star struck Harrow Snr as he rode a bicycle along the drive of the family's country house, killing him instantly ... the incident follows close upon a rumoured split in the Snr Harrow's marriage. At a recent function wife Paula walked out after a disagreement. She is under sedation following the death of her husband. Gerard Harrow, the star's brother, was at home at the time but failed to see the accident. . . .'

A photograph of Gerard with Luke was alongside. As unlike Luke as could be, he was shorter and slim to the point of thinness, but elegantly so. Even in the blurr-edged press picture, the quality of his suit showed, the debonair touch of a pocket handkerchief adding a certain dash to the looks that didn't match his brother's. In each of the photographs on these pages, Luke grew grimmer in a kind of metamorphosis from the candid, smiling young god to the moody man he had become. There was a picture of the family leaving the funeral, a drawn Luke with Gerard and a pretty girl with a frozen face. And another—the first sign of open war between Luke and the press.

'Mr Harrow refused to comment on the finding of accidental death. When asked who would be replacing Harrow Snr as his manager, he hit out at a reporter, striking a tape recorder to the ground. He was restrained by coach Don Marsden, the man most likely to take over the star's management——'

Luke looked violent, his fist upraised—the antithesis of 'Saint' Luke.

'*Harrow trophy*—As a tribute to Gerard "Luke" Harrow, popular figure in the world of tennis, his colleagues have contributed to present the Harrow Cup ... to be awarded each year for a junior competition. It is hoped that his widow, Mrs Paula Harrow will make the first presentation . . .'

Lacey turned the pages to find a later piece that included a snap of Don Marsden performing the duty instead.

She turned back to those earlier pages and smiling studies of Luke with Don Marsden and his father. How alike they were, father and son. What a terrible burden for Luke to bear. An accident that probably plagued him still with all the useless 'if only's'. The pages flipped through her fingers. This was the one. The one that had hurt her enough to send Luke her picture and message of loyalty.

'*Boos for Harrow at Kooyong*—Luke Harrow won his match here today to a cool reception by the crowd. The Melbourne spectators were unusually quiet and there was a chorus of boos when he questioned a line call. Less than six weeks ago the star drove the car that was responsible——'

She closed the scrapbook, took it and put in her car. Later she would read it all again and maybe then she would understand.

On Sunday she lazed in the overgrown back garden with a paperback that failed to grab her, ate a hasty lunch with her parents who were going, they said, to Oran Park.

'But that's the motor racing circuit,' Lacey said, thinking of screaming bikes and roaring crowds.

'That's right. We're meeting a few friends there.'

'What about the noise—won't it affect your ears?' she asked her father who had complained about her radio in past years.

'Pardon?' he cupped one hand around his ear and she laughed at the hoary old joke.

'I fell for it again. Okay, enjoy yourselves. I'll be down again on Friday. Will it be all right if I stay a few nights when I'm working on The Big House next month?'

A bit tricky that, her mother told her, because two of her father's army mates were coming to stay sometime soon. Which was a pity, Lacey thought. She had rather been hoping to avoid any more overnight stays at Fremont.

She was halfway back to Sydney before she thought of it. Paula Harrow didn't appear in any of her scrapbook pictures.

It was several days before she had the estimates ready for Luke.

'I'm staying in town a day or two. Show them to me over dinner at my hotel tonight,' he said with a hint of challenge in his voice. 'It's not far from where you live.'

Hotel? It was tempting. But she held back. She'd allowed her feelings to swamp her, maybe even blind her before, and though she wanted to tell him that he was wrong about Mike, knew it would merely re-open the question of her withdrawal. Coward, she accused herself, you're hiding again, waiting for some sign of his sincerity. With one finger she pushed at her glasses.

'I'm afraid tonight is rather difficult, Luke. Perhaps your office, tomorrow——?'

'No.'

'Well then, will you be at Fremont during the weekend?'

A pause. 'Possibly. What did you have in mind?' A heavy edge of sarcasm there, reminding her of her last time at 'The Big House'.

'I'll be visiting my family for the weekend, Luke.

They live about a half-hour's drive from you so I could call in on Friday evening or Saturday ... unless of course, you'd prefer me to drive down on a week day. ...'

'Saturday,' he said briskly. 'Say, around two. I'm tied up Friday night.'

He was, too. Very attractively tied up with a slender, pretty woman in her early thirties.

'Look, here's your client's picture in the paper,' Janet Teale said at the lunch table on Saturday. '"Mr Luke Harrow, former tennis star with Mrs Leonie Stewart at the champagne supper following the ... at the Opera House ..." mmm. Yes. He's a good-looking man still, isn't he? Remember when you were so mad about him, Lacey—what a wholesome, smiling boy he was.' She shook her head and took a long look at Lacey whose eyes clung to the picture.

No picnics on the Opera House steps for *this* woman. No plastic cups of wine and fish and chips for Leonie Stewart. *Mrs* Leonie Stewart. 'Married or single' his mother had said ... and her own mother's eyes remained a shade anxious.

With ten minutes in hand, Lacey arrived at Fremont. She drove through the gates and along the sweep of drive with a thrill of anticipation. The gardens showed signs of care now. The lawns had recently been cut and the vegetation that had encroached to the drive's edges was trimmed back within its boundaries. Though it was far from its once-famous glamour, the garden was beginning to lose its air of apology. She left her car on the drive at the side of the house and got out to look up at Fremont. The cast iron was gleaming white with new paint and the house looked cleaner, revived.

'I like them,' Luke said when he'd looked through the painstakingly prepared visuals, hand at his chin and an unreadable expression on his face. She was relieved and let out the breath she'd been holding. It was always good to get over the first hurdle, and it had occurred to her that because of her rejection Luke might choose this way to hit back. And how would she have explained that to Mike, who suspected something, but not that she had temporarily lost her senses.

'What's the matter, Lacey? Did you think I might throw a tantrum and chuck your designs out the window?' He put the drawings down and folded his arms.

'It occurred to me,' she admitted.

'Relax. I'm not ready to play the lover scorned.' His mouth set into a straight line and Lacey's wariness increased.

'Did you bring a quote?'

She placed it before him, pointing out its components. He barely skimmed the figures and nodded.

'Hmm. You'd better come upstairs and see what Bartlett's done. He had the thirties renovations ripped out of one bedroom and it might make more difference to your dimensions than we thought.'

A lovely old chimney piece had been revealed and it changed the focus of the entire room. Quickly she drew up another sketch to show him. Luke leaned over her shoulder to look and he was silent for so long that Lacey glanced up at him. He was watching her, not the drawing.

'You'll want a contract signed before you start work,' he said, and she nodded.

'When would be a suitable time?' She took the opportunity to break away from his side to look from the double French doors that opened on to the iron-lace-edged verandah.

Down below were smooth green lawns. A water sprinkler fountained on a glistening patch and the sun struck rainbow colours in the spray.

'My place or yours?' Lacey fumbled with the doorknob, threw open the doors as she felt him draw near with his question.

'Perhaps it would be convenient if I called at your office on Monday?'

He laughed. 'That wasn't what I meant. You look nervous, Lacey. Worried that you might lose your head again and cheat on your partner?' He followed her out on to the verandah, correctly interpreting her professional interest in the view as a retreat. But if she imagined the cooler air and the lack of four walls might be safety, she was wrong.

'Luke, can we just forget that?'

'Oh no,' he caught her arm and she was swung about to face him. 'You told me once you were just good friends. How involved with Logan are you?'

She didn't answer, just shook her head in refusal to discuss it.

'Let me put it to you another way, Lacey——' he jeered softly. 'How badly do you want the contract?'

Her head went back as if he'd hit her. Here was her 'sign' then. Not a sign of the genuine affection she'd hoped from him, but confirmation that he was all his mother had said. Anger blazed from her.

'So she was right. You *are* immoral. Tell me that's a very sick joke, Luke, or I'll tear up my fancy folders full of drawings right now. As far as I'm concerned Logan and Teale can go bankrupt before I'd chase a contract with such zeal. If I'd wanted to use those methods I wouldn't have said no before you signed on the dotted line.' With a rush of strength she wrenched herself from his hold to be free only seconds before he grabbed her again. 'Let me go, you oversized playboy—get someone else to decorate your home and your bed. I can't imagine what ever possessed me to fall for your line in the first place. . . .' She kicked at his shins and connected. Luke swore and hauled her close.

'*Who* said I was immoral?'

'What does it matter? Let me go, you're hurting my arms——'

'Who?' he insisted, shaking her as he had once before. Her glasses jiggled on her nose and she reached up and whipped them off to glare at him.

'If you must know I had it from an unimpeachable source.'

Blue eyes narrowed on her.

'Your mother.'

'My——?' His eyes were those of a child for an instant. Hurt, bewildered. Then chillingly old.

'You must be really something, Luke. A mother doesn't admit such a thing about her son unless——'

'Unless its true?' His voice grated and anger flowed through his hands, clamping them tight about her arms to drag her against him. 'Well, why not? I've worn all the other hats forced on me—why not immoral as well? And since I'm wearing it, I mustn't disappoint my public must I, Lacey?'

Her name was still on his lips as he kissed her, but this was no sweet, seducing caress. This was sheer rage ... a frustrated need to assert masculine superiority ... a punishment. Yet even as she struggled to get away, the tenor altered. Luke gentled, moved his mouth on hers in a sort of entreaty that reached to the core of her. Arms that were a prison a moment before eased about her, his hands moved over her in a silent plea, or so it seemed to Lacey. Her mouth opened to him, and she was more a prisoner now when he showed her his need and not his want. The taunts, the hinted proposition stung her still but Lacey held him tight, her heart twisting at the combined effect of his great strength and his vulnerability. This couldn't be feigned, could it? Questions circled unanswered in her head, faded with the beguilement of his touch. She sighed when he moved his mouth along her jaw and found the sensitive curve of her neck, rested her head against him and pressed a kiss to the base of his throat.

The afternoon breeze played about them, plucking at Lacey's hair and skirt as if to recall her to reality. Her eyes opened. Luke looked down at her for long, quiet seconds while the breeze whispered in the shade trees below and the sprinkler shooshed sideways, scattering its rainbows. As he bent to kiss her again, she glimpsed a movement over his shoulder and her eyes opened wide.

Paula Harrow stood watching them from the next doorway along the verandah and Lacey stiffened, embarrassed at first, then startled by the expression on her face.

'Oh—Luke——' she thrust him away, one hand still clutching her glasses, and stepped back against the iron

lace balustrade, her eyes on the spot where Mrs Harrow
had vanished. Was this another of her fancies
associated with the big, old house? If so it was an odd
one. No ghost this, but a slim woman in a trouser-suit.

'What's the matter—have you suddenly remembered
poor old Mike again?' Luke said roughly and she
started to say that she had seen his mother. Instead she
put her glasses on, wondering if, after all, she had
imagined it. Maybe her mind was providing images to
shock her back to reality, prevent her from making any
more mistakes in the sheltered, confused dream world
of Luke's arms.

'No. Luke, perhaps it would be better if Mike
handled the job for you after all. That is, if you want
Logan and Teale.'

He stuck his hands in his pockets and laughed
harshly. 'Well I want one half of Logan and Teale! But
if its to be strictly business I'll still have *you* work for
me, Lacey. And you'll please me—design-wise I mean,
of course.' He paused, looked out at the garden. The
breeze freshened and lifted the front of his dark blond
hair. He seemed to have forgotten his veiled suggestion
regarding the contract. She didn't remind him. 'Bring
me some alternative colours for this room on
Monday—my office around ten, Lacey,' he said at last.
'I'll sign the contract when I've seen them.'

Downstairs again he opened the side door for her.
'Have you told your boyfriend that I—how shall I
put this—had designs on you?'

'No.'

Mockingly he said: 'Be careful then, Lacey. It's
written all over you.'

She found out what he meant later. Across the rear of
her skirt was a faint impression of Fremont's white iron
lace. She'd forgotten the wet paint ... among other
things.

CHAPTER SIX

LUKE'S secretary phoned to postpone Monday morning's appointment. 'Mr Harrow would like you to see him at his hotel at five.' Lacey wrote down the name and the room number rebelliously. Why couldn't Luke conduct their business in his office or theirs, like any other client? They needed the Harrow job. It was too prestigious to pass up. Lacey would have gladly turned her back on it if it hadn't been for Mike. She had no right to deny the business such a plum. She'd had no right to endanger it right at the start with her starry-eyed idiocy. But that was finished. It was 'strictly business' from now on. All the same, she would ask Mike to go to Luke's hotel this evening instead of her.

'But you have to drive right past the place on your way home,' he pointed out when she told him which hotel.

'I know but—Mike, you did say you hoped I'd call for help,' she reminded him and regretted it instantly. Mike's grey eyes creased in speculation.

'I see.'

'No, you don't.'

'Lacey, I'd like to cover for you but I have a four-thirty appointment at Palm Beach. There's no way I'll get back before six, maybe later.'

It had been worth a try, she thought, wondering what Luke's reaction would have been if Mike had turned up in her place.

'If you like, I'll come down to Fremont with you next time you go,' he offered and she liked the idea. The less she saw of Luke alone, the better.

Don Marsden opened the door of the hotel room. Lacey was immensely relieved that he was there.

'Mr Marsden.'

'Come in. He's in the shower.'

He opened the bar fridge and waved an inviting hand

at the contents, but she shook her head and her eyes went to the door from behind which came the sound of a shower running.

'Lovely weather,' Don said after a minute.

'Yes.'

Raising his glass of beer to her, he drank. He ran a finger across his top lip to remove the foam. 'Working late aren't you, Miss Teale?'

'We decorators are at the beck and call of our customers, Mr Marsden. Luke wanted to sign the contract at five—so here I am.'

'Must play havoc with your personal life. Being at the beck and call, as you say.'

She smiled, met his shrewd, searching eyes directly. 'What exactly do you want to know, Mr Marsden?'

He laughed, took another mouthful of beer. 'Can't fool you can I? Like I said before, Luke's almost a son to me. I just wanted to know a bit about the girl that's got him in such a temper.'

She blinked. Surely Don didn't think Luke's moods were anything to do with her? He was bad-tempered the day she'd met him. The shower had stopped minutes before. Lacey imagined Luke using a towel . . .

'I'm twenty-five and single and like it that way. And I never discuss my personal life with clients. Or coaches,' she smiled. 'Now, could we talk about something else, Mr Marsden?'

'Well, I've tried the weather,' he pointed out. 'Didn't do too good with that.'

Lacey was laughing as Luke emerged from the bathroom, his hair dark and damp, his eyes cool as they rested on her.

'More of your jokes, Don? I hope you told a clean one.'

'Nope. Talking about the weather.' He poured another beer and handed it to Luke. 'It was getting sultry there for a while and I thought summer was here early, but winter just—keeps hanging around.' He downed the last of his drink and dragged a bunch of keys from his pocket. Lacey looked at the signs of departure with dismay. 'Hooroo then. See you at the house tomorrow, Luke. Bye, Miss Teale. Let's hope the weather improves, eh?'

But it wouldn't, Lacey thought, as the door shut behind him. There was a wintry chill in the air as Luke sat down and drew the papers towards him. And she was not feeling exactly summery either. He picked up the pen she had put beside the contract, looked at the colour samples. Then he put them all down again and leaned back in his chair to drink his beer. He stared at her and Lacey viewed this deliberate delay with misgivings.

'When did you speak to my mother?'

'What does it matter?' She certainly wouldn't say it had been during that crucial ten minutes between inviting him to make love to her and refusing him. That could be all too revealing. Her foolhardiness in becoming emotionally involved with him was something to be kept hidden, along with her fourteen-year-old impulsiveness. But at least she'd only given him a photograph that time. Not a real, live offering.

'It must have been that first night you came to Fremont——' he went on, holding her gaze thoughtfully. She looked away and lied.

'Not it wasn't. She spoke to me while you were in the shower the second time I came. While I waited in the study.'

His eyes narrowed as if he was considering the likelihood of that and she added quickly, 'Not that she told me anything I didn't already know.'

Winter blasted her in the face. His blue eyes were glacial. 'You're pretty damned sure about me signing this, aren't you?' He waved a hand at the contract papers, and her mouth went dry.

'No.'

'What would your partner say if you didn't get it after all? Would you tell him that you lost it because you played the tease with a client?'

She shook her head. 'That's not true, Luke.'

He leaned forward and set his glass down, keeping his hand around it as he watched her. 'Such a cool lady ... but I only have to touch you to get a response. If I came over there now and made love to you, you'd be putty in my hands.'

Her body was weakening even at the words. Pulse rushing, breath suddenly constricted she looked at him, her lips slightly parted as if he was already near enough to kiss her. The bland music played. Through the window beyond Luke, the first city and harbour lights gleamed in the dusk. It was five-thirty and the sun had set, leaving just the fading colours of its warmth. Abruptly she pressed her mouth closed and tried to be the 'cool lady' he'd mentioned. Her hand raised to her glasses.

'You'll see that I've already signed the documents. As you requested, they cover the first stages only. As soon as we have this more urgent work underway, I'll prepare designs and estimates on the remainder of the house.'

'Sidestepping again,' he said, and picked up the pen to turn it between his fingers. 'But you're not out of the woods yet, Lacey.'

She didn't ask him what he meant. All she wanted was to walk out of here with the signed contract in her hand. His signature went on and she took Logan and Teale's copy.

'Work will commence on Thursday, Luke. If you have any queries or further suggestions, just phone. Mike and I are, of course, available at any time to keep you informed.'

'That's good of you, Miss Teale,' he mocked her professional manner. 'Thank you *so* much for calling by. My apologies for not keeping our appointment this morning.'

A flash of irritation showed in her eyes at his tongue-in-cheek apology. He had obviously altered the arrangements so that she would have to come here where 'strictly business' was harder to maintain.

'Quite all right.' She was moving to the door, had almost made it before he got up and strode over to place his palm flat against it in a blocking gesture. Not out of the woods yet, she thought and swallowed. Unexpectedly he held out his hand and she placed hers in it, thinking that a handshake with Luke was the ultimate irony after those passionate clinches they'd shared.

'Goodnight, Lacey——' he tugged on her arm and she stumbled against him.

'Strictly business you said,' Lacey gasped. He was right. She *was* putty in his hands.

'Did I?' he breathed in her ear. 'Never trust the word of an immoral man.'

She held her attaché case and her free hand against his chest with every intention of pushing him away. But his skin was warm beneath the thin shirt and he smelled clean and soapy and her lips parted again as she looked at that sensuous cynic's mouth so close.

'You look warm, Lacey,' he murmured and his hand went beneath her suit jacket to her breast. Her quick, indrawn breath brought a smile of satisfaction to his face. Lacey forced herself to stay there, stifling the surges of pleasure from the expert movement of those long, strong fingers on her. Kitchens, she thought in desperation as she had once before in his arms. Prosaic kitchens and bathrooms were the things to concentrate on—her least favourite rooms and the ones on which she necessarily had to work harder. When he kissed her, she kept her eyes open and her mouth still—a stainless steel kitchen sink ... she conjured up the image as Luke's tongue flicked around her lips, probed for a weakness ... a *double* stainless steel sink ... he drew her closer and her attaché case bumped his knee and swung back and forth in her grip. Luke ran one hand over her back into its lower curve and moulded the other over her hip. Kitchens, she thought again despairingly ... garbage disposal units. . . .

His look of satisfaction had gone when he stopped. Lacey stepped back, ran a hand over her hair and spoke as if the last few minutes hadn't happened.

'Goodnight, Luke.'

He said nothing, but there was frustration in his abrupt pull on the door and anger in the slam of it behind her.

'Everything okay?' Mike asked meaningfully when she presented the contract to him the next day.

'Just fine.' Saved by a double stainless steel sink, she thought wryly. When she went down to Fremont on Thursday, Mike went with her. She told him it wasn't necessary, fairly certain now that any personal by-play between her and Luke was at an end, but Mike insisted.

'After all, if I haven't seen the place I won't be much help to you if you strike a problem, will I?' She felt like saying that any design problems would be pure delight compared to the one major mistake that was a weeping thundercloud over her head.

Mrs Simmons let them in. Luke was there in white tennis clothes and her heart did a quick dance.

'How old is he?' Mike asked in an undertone as they waited for Luke to come down the stairs.

'Thirty-four.'

'Hmmmph. He certainly looks good for his age,' he said grudgingly.

'You should be pleased. It proves that all does not crumble away at thirty,' she said lightly and turned her mind to garbage disposal units.

Luke greeted them with distant courtesy, shook hands with Mike and gave her what could be described as a smile. He walked with them for a time while Mike viewed the house and kept up the Logan and Teale end of the conversation.

'Lacey's combing Sydney for a gasolier for this room,' he said, looking up at the dining-room ceiling which had been fitted in pre-war years with a dreadful shaded pendant affair. 'Of course we'll convert it to electricity.' Putting an arm around her shoulders, he said to Luke: 'We'll really enjoy working on your house Mr Harrow and I can modestly say that Lacey and I make a great team. You won't be disappointed. Will he, partner?' Mike gave an intimate little squeeze to her shoulder as period to that. Luke's eyes flicked from him to Lacey where they lingered. His mouth was harsh.

'Won't I?' he murmured and made abrupt excuses to leave them with Mrs Simmons for the upstairs tour.

'For goodness sake, Mike,' Lacey said as they drove away from Fremont's newly renovated iron gates, 'Why do you keep acting as if we're more than business partners? It isn't very professional.' What a laugh. Her chiding someone else for unprofessional behaviour!

'You called for help,' he reminded her. 'I thought that was the kind you needed.'

'Well it isn't. You misunderstood.'

Mike didn't seem convinced, but he let the matter drop.

The Harrow job ushered in a new frantic quality to Lacey's life. She worked on the first stage installation while preparing the second and coped with her other clients as well. Mrs Prentiss was kept at bay with the promise of the newest samples of pink upholstery fabric the moment they arrived from the mills and she delegated any new work to Mike. Somehow she managed to fit in her monthly article for the magazine that had featured her bedroom designs. During the next month she made numerous trips to Fremont and each time refused Luke's terse request to stay over, driving back to town late or staying at her parents' house which, as yet, had not been crowded with the arrival of her father's mates.

'Are you—involved with Luke Harrow?' Beth asked outright one night as she watched Lacey lapse into pensiveness over the Fremont layout.

'Involved.' Lacey said carefully after a moment. 'What a lovely, all-purpose word. Why do you ask?'

'Oh—probably because you must be seeing him a lot but never mention him. Have you ever noticed that people talk a lot about friends and acquaintances but when it's someone who really matters they kind of— clam up?'

Lacey kept her eyes down. 'Very profound. No, I've never noticed.'

Beth brought her some coffee. 'Take a break, Lacey—you're working yourself to death. Come to a movie with me. We haven't done that for ages.'

Lacey smiled and took off her glasses. 'You're right. I don't think I can manage the movie but,' she paused, '—would you object if I threw a party here for Mike?'

'A party?' Beth's smiled stiffened. 'Why, what's Mike been doing that needs celebrating?'

'He'll be thirty in a couple of weeks and he's been a bit moody about it. I thought a surprise party might cheer him up.'

'Oh sure, that'd be fun. I'll—er—stay home and help on the night if you like,' she offered in an offhand manner.

'Would you?' Lacey said earnestly.

'Is he worried about turning thirty then?'

'Dead depressed. I think Mike sees life slipping away from him. He keeps telling me how lonely he is upstairs in his flat and when I point out that he is rather accomplished and not entirely derelict financially, he shrugs it off. Mike is at the dangerous age for a man when he starts to wonder just what life is all about.'

'I didn't think he worried about anything. He always looks so cool.'

Lacey shrugged. 'You never can tell.'

'Anyway, I thought you and he might consolidate the partnership one of these days.' Beth inspected the leaves of her football boot pothos, her neck and shoulders ostentatiously unconcerned.

'Wrong again,' Lacey said lightly. 'You don't know much about Mike, do you, considering he's been dropping in ever since we started sharing. Whenever I mention him you kind of—um—clam up.'

The strain began to tell on Lacey. 'Strictly business' was difficult when she had to face up to Luke several times a week only to find that in spite of everything, he still moved her. His face was bleak these days and he snapped out complaints that were not always justified, tied up a great deal of her time in checking out details that were perfectly in order, and generally gave her a hard time.

When she was in Sydney, he would phone and bark out a demand to have something completed faster than originally planned. When she was at Fremont he would ask about something that could only be checked in Sydney. His attitude seemed consistent with the thwarted pettiness of a man who had put in considerable effort and failed to claim his reward. And yet there was that something about him that reached her regardless of the sergeant-major monosyllables and sarcastic references to Mike. It only seemed to make him more snappish than ever when she refused to be baited and dealt with his tyranny with tight-reined calm. But Lacey knew she was at her limits. Every day her grip on the reins loosened and when she let go. . . . 'You'll please me . . .' he'd said with that sardonic smile when she'd leapt from his arms on the verandah. But ⸮r professional manner was tried to its limits by Luke's ⸮nds. As the first deadline approached she was tired and ⸮y, a condition brought on by overwork and the contin⸮al battle with her emotions.

'I want you here for the next three days until my brother arrives,' he told her abruptly one afternoon as she was leaving the chaos of the entrance hall. It was almost at the end of its restoration to Owen Bartlett's specifications. New, etched glass had been manufactured and fitted to the boarded-up windows and the oak dado and filler panelling had been replaced. But the painters and paperhangers had yet to finish the transformation.

'That won't be necessary, Luke,' she told him, crushing her anger at his peremptory tone. 'The work is under control and will be finished on time. I will, of course, be down again on Friday to check the final details.'

'Not good enough, Lacey. I told you at the outset that I wanted full supervision of the work. There have been a few glaring errors that you could have forestalled had you stayed over as I stipulated.'

There *had* been some ridiculous delays in the last few days. Silly things had happened—mistakes by contractors, items misplaced, paint spilled—deliveries made and unaccountably missing for hours only to turn up somewhere unexpected. Silly, trifling things that made Logan and Teale look like a tinpot operation. But none of them that Lacey could see, could have been prevented by her staying here overnight.

'You're being unreasonable, Luke,' she managed to say mildly, but her temper was holding on a thread.

He put his hands on his hips and glared at her. 'And you're being inefficient. Inefficient and unprofessional.'

She went scarlet. The thread snapped. 'You'll have your rooms ready for the weekend, Luke. Don't worry. If I have to carpet the floors myself and haul the furniture upstairs, they'll be ready. And maybe, just maybe, we wouldn't *be* behind on the schedule if you hadn't wasted my time and the contractors' with your childish, spoiled boy antics. . . .'

His head flung back and his eyes narrowed. 'Just be careful what you say, Lacey——'

'Why?' She took off her glasses and her green eyes flashed with the accumulated anger and frustration of the last month. 'Do you intend to wield this job of yours as the ultimate weapon again? Do you imagine that I'm prepared to do anything for it, Luke? Sleep with you—crawl—be a doormat for your boorish bad temper and foul moods? A contract cuts *both* ways, Mr Harrow. If these are the conditions under which I'm supposed to work, you can take the contract for the rest of the house and—and stuff it in that practice ball machine of yours.'

She stuck her glasses back on and turned on her heel to stalk outside, her feet scrunching on the new gravel that surfaced the drive, but she didn't reach her car. His steps gritted behind her but even as she hurried a hand grasped her left arm and she was brought up sharply so that she all but overbalanced. 'Now hear this, Lacey, and hear it good,' he hissed in her ear. 'Be down here not just for the next three days but at least three out of every week afterwards and nurse this work along or . . .'

'Or what, Luke?' she snapped, her teeth clenched so tight that her jaw hurt.

'Or I just might be forced to bring legal proceedings against Logan and Teale Interiors for inability to fill their contract.'

'That would never hold up and you know it, Luke. The delays have been minor. No court would rule that we weren't fulfilling our promises.'

'Maybe not,' he said harshly. 'But the publicity wouldn't do you and your boyfriend any good, would it? Logan and Teale Interiors tossed out by former tennis star, Luke Harrow . . . you must know that anything I say will be seized on by the press. They've been waiting for me to say something for ten years. Of course none of it need be true. But the papers give generous space to speculation. I know. I can afford to sue and lose, Lacey—can you afford to be sued and win?'

The enormity of it hit her. He could ruin them. Everything she and Mike had built up since combining their single careers as consultants. The bank loan was still to be paid off, this year's tax loomed over them ... but while their reputation bloomed they could look forward to prosperity. That was all they had really, she thought—their reputation.

'I don't believe you would be so vindictive——'

'You and your partner will make a neat little profit from me, Lacey, and I want value for money.'

She twitched her glasses off again with a hand that shook from rage and fear. 'Then you'll get it, Mr Harrow. At what time would you like me to report as whipping boy?'

He didn't answer, merely looked at her. His chest rose and fell sharply, his face cooled from anger to settle into the bleak lines that moved her even now when she could almost hate him.

'You'll get no complaints if the job is done properly,' he said tautly.

'The job *is* being done properly and your complaints aren't justified. Well, maybe I won't feel the need to be fair either if this is a sample of what I can expect. I may not have your clout, but I have a few friends in the press.' She turned away, bit her tongue in instant regret. What a *stupid* thing to say. After her years of careful discretion with clients, to even suggest such a thing— especially with this man. Luke crowded her as she reached her car and opened the door.

'Don't try it, Lacey,' he warned with steel in his voice and she schooled her face to look up at him. Her voice wasn't so easily controlled. There was a distinct wobble in it.

'My apologies. Naturally I wouldn't break my rule of confidentiality. I'm afraid I let my temper get the better of me. I'll be here in the morning.'

She got in, performed all the familiar motions with jerky movements. Luke leaned forward, a hand on the window ledge. 'Lacey——' he said in a different tone and followed it with something else. But she shot forward along the glittering new gravel drive and out on to the tree-lined road.

How could she tell Mike that she had put their business in jeopardy by allowing her heart to rule her head for a few crazy days? There was no way out now. They were committed to the job and she had to toe the line or not only she, but Mike would suffer too. Luke could demand anything of her now she realised—could run her around in circles until she dropped. Lacey wished passionately that she could run away some-where—remove herself from Luke's reach—forget it all. But she knew there was no such place—and no such thing.

She stopped the car under a poplar tree and did something she hadn't done for years. She cried.

Lacey was not in the mood for the arrangements for Mike's surprise party when she got home. But it was Tuesday and the party was planned for Friday and the flat was in its usual state with Beth's belongings scattered, hung and draped all about. Now that she had to be away until the party there was nothing for it but to bring forward their Wednesday night cleaning. How the place would remain tidy until Friday was something she didn't dwell on too much.

When they had cleaned up and eaten, they checked their party supplies, the cake candles, the guest list.

'How are you going to get him here, Lacey?'

'Oh, I casually suggested he might like to drop in and have a quiet meal and a drink. He always seems to like coming here.'

'He might go out and celebrate with some mates—or a girlfriend.'

'No. I've been in touch with his male friends. And he hasn't had a girlfriend since he broke up months ago with Roz.'

'He's had you.'

'I've been a stopgap for Mike. We dated a few times

... he needed to feel attached to someone I think ... anyone. He's more a brother to me if he's honest about it.' Her mind went guiltily to the danger she had created for Mike. Turning thirty would be the least of his troubles if Luke implemented his threat. But he wouldn't, surely. Would he? Her instincts told her no. But then, they'd been wrong before.

She said nothing of it to Mike but explained that she was needed at Fremont until Friday. 'I'll be staying over at my parents' place.'

'I see.' He relaxed at that and she was immediately irritated at whatever jealousy or possessiveness prompted it.

'You're leaving me at the mercy of Mrs Prentiss again,' he complained. 'I see what you mean about her. Even her hair is pink.'

'Sorry,' she smiled. 'Don't forget, we're having dinner and drinks on Friday night to celebrate your passing from youth to middle age.'

'Right little morale booster, aren't you? Where—your place or mine?'

'Mine of course. But I promise to be good. Stroganoff, Rachmaninov and naturally, hands off,' she said tongue-in-cheek.

'Now hang on ...' he called after her as she left, 'about that last bit. ...'

Just as she had anticipated, she had a great deal of time on her hands at Fremont once she had checked out the work still being done on the guest bedroom and adjoining bathroom suite. It irked her to be caged here while her desk in the office remained piled high with work requiring her attention. But she had brought some of it with her and she went in search of Luke to request somewhere she could work. There was no trace of him either downstairs or up and she slipped into a bathroom to freshen up before searching any further. Her mother wouldn't be too happy when she saw her tonight. The shadows persisted under her eyes, so she dabbed a touch of make-up on as camouflage and renewed the lipstick that had somehow disappeared while she talked to the contractors. She looked at herself critically for a few moments, fiddled with the high neckline of her tan dress. It was a long time since she had moaned over her too-wide mouth and the nose that had tilted instead of growing arrow straight. Once over the uncertainties of adolescence, Lacey has accepted herself and appreciated the good things . . . the fine skin and strong-coloured eyes, and her natural streaky blondeness which cost many of her brown-haired friends a fortune in hairdressing fees. Now she saw the uncertainty in her eyes again. Not for the way she looked—but for the way she felt. Hoisting her bag over her shoulder, she opened the door. She had managed to get over the disappointment of not having an arrow-straight nose, so perhaps in time she would get over this new wave of discontent.

As if to prove her wrong she ran directly into Luke as she emerged into the wide hall. He was hurrying, stripping off a t-shirt as he walked. It was half over his head when they collided and he steadied her with the shirt still twined about one arm. There was a glow about him from exercise. His bare torso had a faint sheen and Lacey could feel his heat. Disentangling herself she stepped away from the disturbing masculine ambience heightened by his half-naked body. Heart pounding every bit as hard as the carpet layers' hammers just along the hall, she thought how naive she was to have likened the feeling she had for Luke as discontent. It was a total eclipse. She ran a tongue over her lips and glanced up at him.

'Tempted, Lacey?' he asked softly, seeing the nervous movement.

His accuracy bothered her—the sneer on his fine-cut mouth hurt. Lacey lifted her head a little higher. Client or no client, she would fight back. After what he'd said yesterday it really didn't seem to matter if she combated his rudeness with like. She let her eyes run down over his magnificent physique. Damp, gold-flecked hair covered his deep chest and funnelled downwards to the band of his shorts, emerged again on muscular legs.

'No thanks. Macho is over-rated.'

'It was certainly rating pretty well with you for a time. Until you remembered you already *had* a partner.'

She shifted her gaze from his face to the base of his throat. Not a lot of help as it turned out. She remembered pressing her mouth to his skin ... just there. ...

'I was looking for you,' she said jerkily.

'Well,' he spread his arms and his chest muscles rippled. 'You've found me.'

Stoically she went on as if he was four-foot-nothing dressed in a pin-striped suit instead of what Beth had called a 'hunk'.

'My supervision of your work is not exactly an all-day job right now. I need somewhere to do some paperwork.'

'Use my study. I won't be requiring it today. You brought an overnight bag I hope.'

'Yes, of course. Your—request was quite plain, Luke. I'll be staying over——'

He nodded and began to move away.

'—however, not here.' He turned back, irritation flaring in his blue eyes. 'But I will be on your doorstep tomorrow as early as if I was. As I told you, my parents live nearby and naturally they wish me to stay with them.'

There was a thwarted silence. Lacey wondered if he had some secondary motive for wanting her here overnight. The original one perhaps?

'Naturally.' He tossed his damp shirt over one shoulder and walked away, giving her an impressive view of his back. 'Don't leave this afternoon without seeing me.'

He was gone for most of the day, for which Lacey was thankful. Mid-afternoon she heard his voice again somewhere in the house and her nerves tightened with his presence. It was after five when she checked out the job's progress and prepared to leave. As she gathered up her papers and returned them to her attaché case, Luke's mother entered the study.

She greeted her a little self-consciously, recalling that

Paula Harrow had last seen her with Luke on the upstairs verandah. The woman smiled and Lacey thought maybe she had imagined the expression on her face that day. Anger—disapproval—neither fitted it exactly. It was more than that she thought uneasily. But Luke's mother didn't mention it or renew her warnings. It was possible that she hadn't recognised the girl being kissed by her son. Dryly, Lacey acknowledged that they probably all looked the same to Paula Harrow.

'Miss Teale—you've done a wonderful job on the dining room and the guest bedroom is going to be charming. What a talented girl you are.'

It was mollifying after Luke's bad-tempered reception of all her efforts.

'Thank you, Mrs Harrow. Would you know where Luke is? He wanted me to see him before I leave.'

'Down at the courts, I daresay,' she returned, her eyes wandering about the room. 'What do you have in mind for this room, Miss Teale?'

Lacey thought it a little strange that Luke wouldn't have told her, but she obliged.

'. . . and I've located a superb desk that was made about the same time that this house was built.'

'Surely this one is perfectly good?' Paula Harrow said, running a hand over the smooth surface.

'Yes, it is a lovely piece and will fit very well in one of the bedrooms as a bureau. The one that will go in here will suit Luke perfectly because it was built for a left-handed owner.' She smiled. 'It's really quite unusual.'

'Luke isn't left-handed,' his mother said. 'He's used this desk for years——' Once again she touched the timber edge and Lacey stared. 'Now when do you think we can have a talk about my suite, Miss Teale?'

'Oh—I'll bring some of our display photographs and samples from Sydney next week, Mrs Harrow and perhaps I can come and take a look at your rooms?'

'That sounds fine, but leave your measuring and so on until after my son's visit. I hope you'll meet Gerry, Miss Teale. He's a clever man, the youngest to be appointed to his position with the Commission in

London.' She sighed. 'Gerry's a rarity these days. Brains, culture and good looks.'

'He sounds the perfect son,' Lacey said diplomatically and Paula Harrow smiled.

'He is.'

Lacey went out into the hall thoughtfully. Just what kept Mrs Harrow in poor health? Such poor health that she failed to remember that her second son was one of the world's most famous left-handers?

Don Marsden came out of the coach-house as she went to the courts. Luke was down there, opposite the ball machine and the regular pop of balls spitting out and the crack of Luke's returns carried on the afternoon air.

'When am I going to get decorated?' Don asked, as he stood there brushing a sports shoe.

'That depends, Mr Marsden,' she said gravely. 'Have you acted above and beyond the call of duty lately?'

'Ah. Quick aren't you?' he grinned. 'The old house is starting to look really something. I like your ideas.'

'You didn't think you would, Mr Marsden.'

'Yeah. Well, we all make mistakes. Call me Don.'

That meant, she imagined, that she had passed some test.

'Okay, Don. Call me Lacey. Once the work is underway in the remainder of the house I'll begin on the coach-house.' She glanced at the building materials and scaffolding that was erected around the far end of the old stables.

'Want to have a look now?' he invited and she went in to discover an untidy, cosy set of rooms that had been clumsily partitioned sometime in the thirties or forties judging by the materials. But the original walls with their stone and timber trims, the beamed roof, gave the place a rough, warm character.

'A bit messy,' Don apologised. 'My wife used to keep me tidy but she died fifteen years ago. Since then,' he shook his head, 'I just never learned how to be neat.'

'Is this your wife?' she asked, pointing to a large, framed photograph.

'That's her.'

Her eyes moved along the dresser, drawn by other photographs. Luke in action, Luke fierce with concentration waiting to receive, Luke holding trophies with his arm around Don and with the older man who looked so very like him. She knew she shouldn't stop to look at them but couldn't pass them by. 'His father?' she asked, even though she knew. 'They're very alike.'

Don gave a grunt of laughter. 'In looks, that was about all.'

'They were close?'

'Yeah. Close. People got the idea that the boy needed Luke but if you ask me, it was more the other way.'

'What do you mean—the boy——?'

'Luke—oh I see what you're getting at. His dad was "Luke" too.'

'I thought his name was Gerard?' 'Gerard Lucas' it said in her scrapbook cuttings. And each name perpetuated in a son. Don gave her a shrewd look from under shaggy brows grey-bleached from the sun.

'Don't miss much do you? Yeah, his name was Gerard but he liked to be called by his second name.'

Lacey changed the subject, not liking that look in Don's eye. She didn't want to be caught as a once-avid fan of Luke's.

'Do you live here all the time, Don?'

He shook his head. 'Got a house in Gosford.'

'The one decorated by the pretty young fellow?'

Don chuckled at that. 'That's the one.'

They went outside. The tennis ball machine was still making its champagne cork popping noises.

'Luke's mother seems very nice,' she said, looking at the man on the court. 'What's the matter with her health?'

'So you've met her have you? Hmmm.' Don picked up the other tennis shoe and began brushing it off. 'She's a bit on the nervy side.'

'Has she had a breakdown?' Lacey asked, as bluntly as Don.

'What makes you think that?' he shot back.

'Oh—nothing. She just looks so well, yet Mrs Simmons said she has bad health, so I thought——'

'Just nerves,' Don nodded. 'Her doctor was a bit surprised that she had a bit of a turn when they moved here. But she's okay. Goes into town occasionally but keeps to the house a lot.'

'She seems very proud of her older son. Gerard.' Luke ran across the court, jumped over the net and went to adjust the machine.

'Hmmph. Yeah—he's a bright boy all right is our Gerard. Paula always favoured him. Funny how people fawn over them that do nothing for them and bite the hand that feeds them . . .' he muttered and looked at Luke who jumped the net again and prepared to receive volleys. Don seemed about to say more and changed his mind. 'He won't be long now. Go on down and wait for him. If he hadn't retired, you'd have to pay to watch him.'

She did stay for a time, but where Luke couldn't see her. In the end she went back to the house to await his dismissal. It cost rather too much to watch him.

CHAPTER SEVEN

On Thursday the pace quickened. Workmen and cleaners were everywhere. Luke snapped and frowned and Lacey, observing him, tried to fathom the reason for his increasing unreason. He had been like this that first time she met him in his office, yet afterwards, for those few incredible days, he had let her see another side of him.

There was no trace of it now, she reflected, eyes on his tense, scowling face. All that charm and boyish confidentiality had been a superb act. He looked up, caught her attention on him and if anything, his tension increased. But he turned away, striding from the room and in a moment or two his mother came in to ask Lacey's recommendation about the flowers for Gerard's suite.

'I'll order them,' she smiled, obviously happy at the coming visit of her older son. Then she too went out. Lacey went to work in the study again, suddenly struck by the fact that she had never actually seen Luke and his mother together. Still, it was a big house. . . . At the desk she answered the telephone automatically and blandly took a message from Leonie Stewart for Luke.

'Tell him to ring me tonight at home would you? He knows my number.'

'Certainly, Mrs Stewart.' She visualised the slim, attractive woman whose picture had appeared with Luke's in the newspaper. Perhaps *she* would lift the temper from his face.

Certainly no-one else did. Not even Don Marsden with whom she'd seen Luke laughing a number of times before this new surge of churlishness. In fact she came upon them exchanging strong words and before she could discharge her message, Luke strode away, the lines on his face etched harsher than ever. Don glanced at her and gave an expressive shrug but his brow was furrowed. Or Harrowed, Lacey thought.

'You might be decorated sooner than you think,' she said in an attempt at lightness. 'If you tangle with Luke in this mood it's definitely beyond the call of duty. But it could be a posthumous decoration.'

'I told him it was a bloody silly idea to have them here . . .' he muttered, one weathered hand massaging the back of his neck.

'Who? His brother and his wife? Is that why he's so moody?'

Another assessing glance from beneath those thick brows alerted Lacey. 'Don't they get on—Luke and his brother?'

'Well——' Don chewed at his lip, rubbed his chin between forefinger and thumb, 'They used to be real close but—well dammit, I don't see why you shouldn't know. Ruth, Gerry's wife, was all but engaged to Luke at one time.'

It all started to make sense. Here, maybe, was the answer to Luke's radical change ten years ago. She knew there had to be some other factor. Her heart knocked a few times and began a downward slide.

'Before the accident?'

'Yeah. Crazy about him she was—and he about her. But Ruthie, it turned out, was more in love with the public image than the man. And his image slipped after the accident. She liked the idea of being Mrs Saint Luke with the world smiling on him. But she didn't fancy being in the devil's court.' The phrase rippled along Lacey's spine. The devil's court. . . .

'And Gerry, tipped to take up a diplomatic post overseas would be very attractive to someone with ambitions . . .' she thought aloud, conscious of a certain unfairness to the unknown Ruth. She was jealous of a name. But Don had been there. If he said that Ruth had thrown over Luke for Gerry then she must have done so, though Lacey found it hard to imagine a woman falling out of love with Luke because of the scandal. What additional hurt had that caused him, on top of his father's death?

'Now how did you know about his posting abroad?' Don asked, eyes narrowed again. 'You seem to be damned well informed.'

'His mother mentioned a few things about Gerry, and I put two and two together,' she claimed quickly. Don seemed to accept that. He looked anxious, obviously about his 'boy'.

'Gerry and Luke used to be great pals in spite of the age difference but—they went their separate ways and if you ask me, they should keep it that way. I thought he'd come to terms with it now——' he muttered.

'Does Luke still—love her then? Ruth?' she asked. It would explain a lot. Why he had a succession of woman and why his mother said he was 'immoral'. Perhaps he had to prove to himself over and over that they weren't worth it. She discarded the melodramatic idea as Don glared at her.

'Of course he doesn't!' he said a bit too forcefully. 'He's a decent boy—wouldn't let himself feel that way about a girl married to his own brother!'

But he mightn't be able to help himself, Lacey thought.

'Don't know what he's trying to prove—but he shouldn't have them here . . . I told him so. . . .'

Estranged from his brother, perhaps still emotionally attached to his brother's wife . . . it was hardly surprising that Luke was under a strain at their impending visit. But knowing that didn't help her much. His attitude was so abrasive and her own emotions so torn, that no amount of understanding could keep her tongue gentle and she had one or two skirmishes with him before she went home to her parents' place on Thursday night.

'I have a message for you, Luke,' she said coolly. 'Mrs Stewart would like you to call her at home tonight. She said you had her number.'

Hard blue eyes bored into hers. She had an urge to reach out and smooth away the lines on his face, coax some warmth into his eyes. He looked so tired. So bitter.

'Good. I could do with something pleasant right now.'

The remark was so unfair that her sympathy was

wiped out. 'Couldn't we all. Let's just hope that Mrs
Stewart can soothe the angry beast and maybe the rest
of us will benefit.'

A muscle moved in his cheek. 'You could be lucky.
Leonie has a very—soothing manner.'

'Wonderful. Perhaps you should get *her* to occupy
the small guest room. A soothing presence around here
is sorely needed.'

'Your Dad's mates are coming next week, Lacey,' her
mother told her over breakfast on Friday. 'So I'm
afraid we'll have to give your old room to Archie.'

'Sure. I expected that. There's no need for me to stay
over next week anyway.' And what Luke didn't know
wouldn't hurt him. She could make the long drive back
to Sydney each night and set out early every morning to
arrive just as if she'd been staying a stone's throw from
Fremont. She grimaced. The morning trip could take
two hours. It would be tiring but better than provoking
another row over his notions of 'supervision'.

The next morning the ornaments and small fittings
arrived from Sydney and the guest bedroom suite was a
mass of shredded paper, tissue and cartons. In the
bathroom a carpenter was fitting towel rails and the
specially manufactured shower screen that she had
commissioned to blend with the lofty, spacious
Victorian proportions. Leaning on the mantel in the
bedroom was a superb, carved-framed mirror ready for
hanging on the hook already installed and Lacey
considered it carefully, hoping her decision on its height
had been correct. Without thinking, she lifted it, sliding
its heavy weight up the wall, to see how it would look
but couldn't push it high enough to reach the hook. The
thing weighed a ton—she should have known better
than to touch it. Worse, she discovered that while she
could hold it up, it was too heavy to lower gently and
her fingers would be trapped underneath if she tried it.

'Damn,' she said under her breath and tried shifting
her hands to the sides, but the weight tipped and she
only just stopped it from falling altogether. She was just
about to call for the carpenter's help when Luke's
image appeared in the silvered glass. Immediately she

tried to look in control, her fingers aching to support the mirror against the wall. After all his bad-tempered accusations of inefficiency she didn't want to invite any more of his scathing criticism for risking a valuable item. He would go in a minute and then she would call for help.

'Is this chaos going to be resolved into some sort of order by one o'clock?' he rasped from the doorway. 'There are some cleaners coming in.'

Lacey watched him in the mirror.

'Oh dear, you don't seem to have benefited from Mrs Stewart's soothing manner,' she said before she could stop herself. All night the picture of him rushing to the arms of the slim, pretty woman had haunted her. She was almost pleased that his mood was as irascible as yesterday. It would have been salt in the wound to have him mellow and smiling as a result of Leonie Stewart's ministrations.

'I would have. But work tied me up.' He came further into the room, hands on hips. She almost forgot the ache in her fingers at the sight of his unsmiling, handsome face—the tense, harsh outline of his shoulders. Love and need stabbed through her in a piercing pain. As he came closer her body stiffened.

'Pity,' she said. 'You need an antidote of some kind.' The mirror began to move and this time she couldn't stop it. Luke's image blurred as it slid sideways. He came up behind her, reached past and supported the mirror, an arm either side of her. Lacey felt the stretch of his muscles as he pushed upwards, then down until the frame slipped over the hook. The mantel's marble pressed against her breasts, striking cold through the thin silk of her blouse while his warmth so close behind her spread like fire through her body. Instead of moving away, he stayed there, hands on the mantel shelf trapping her, and Lacey felt his breath warm and fast on her neck. Her eyes clung to his in the glass.

'An antidote,' he murmured. 'A dose of the poison itself. That's just what I need.' He lowered his head to the curve of her neck and shoulder and pressed a kiss there through the thin material, his eyes never leaving hers in the glass.

Lacey's lids dropped a fraction as the sensation shot through her. A dose of the poison—that's what women were to Luke ... antidote to Ruth ... but her heart began a heavy pounding at his touch and this time she had left it too late to set her mind to work on prosaic things to block him out. Very deliberately, still watching her, he lifted a hand and pushed aside the collar of her shirt. Then his lips touched burningly on her skin. A quick intake of breath gave her away. Luke smiled, a sardonic twist of the lips that struck at her. Her escape was foiled as he edged closer, forcing her against the fireplace, imprisoned by his arms raised to the shelf. All along her back and thighs she felt the imprint of Luke's hard body and it was all she could do to bring any words to mind to break his sensuous spell.

'Haven't you forgotten your Mrs Stewart?' she chided, eyes on his in the mirror.

'Haven't you forgotten poor old Mike?' he murmured. 'Again?'

'No,' she said flatly, but watched in fascination as he angled his head to press his mouth against the hollow of her cheek. She should move, but she was unable to draw her eyes from this picture of him making love to her, framed to keep. Luke's arms went around his midriff, pulling her back from the marble's chill to her heat and his hand closed over her breast. Her heart pounded in his palm. He fondled, squeezed the soft flesh to make the beat faster still, and smiled at her reaction written clear on her face for him to see.

'You still want me, Lacey.'

'No,' she denied futilely while her body was saying something else.

'Liar,' he said softly and was turning her unresisting body to face him when the carpenter emerged from the adjoining bathroom.

'About the position of those . . .' he began and blinked as Lacey stepped quickly away from Luke's embrace. When she finished talking to the man Luke was gone and she went to straighten the mirror, thinking how very wistful she looked framed in it alone—and how very big a space was left beside her without Luke.

Later she made a tedious journey back along the Hume Highway to the city to locate several paintings which had not turned up at Fremont. The dealer assured her that they had been collected by the delivery van the previous day but her search at the big house revealed no trace of them. In desperation she visited a small gallery run by a long-time business friend and went away with three works that would fill the spaces allotted for the others until they were found. She stopped to make a quick phone call to Beth at work to let her know that she might be running late for Mike's party.

'He'll be coming over around seven. Just start without me.'

'But we can't do that,' Beth objected.

'Well you certainly can't keep fifteen guests hidden in my bedroom for an indefinite time.'

'Ooh, yes—see what you mean,' Beth giggled. 'Okay, leave it to me.'

'Those aren't the paintings I chose,' Luke said when he walked with her on a final inspection of the finished rooms that evening. Painstakingly she explained— apologised. 'These are temporary replacements until I can track down the others.'

'You drove back to town for these?'

'Of course,' she said crisply, keeping her eyes away from the mirror as if this morning's reflections might not yet have faded from its surface. 'We wouldn't want to be sued for not fulfilling our contract.'

There was a silence and Lacey regretted bringing that threatening subject up again.

'Could we speed this up a little, Luke?' she asked politely. 'I have a party to go to tonight.'

She couldn't interpret the look he gave her. It had a little anger, frustration and the wintry bleakness that moved her as it always did. But it was more likely, she decided, just irritation that she should consider anything but working for him of any importance.

He went on through the cleaned suite of rooms. The smell of new carpet and fabric hung about them, the great antique brass bed gleamed, the mirror tossed back a reflection no more disturbing this time than the flowers that Paula Harrow had arranged and placed on the mantel. At length he looked broodingly at her and said, 'It looks great, Lacey. You've done a fine job.'

After the past weeks the compliment made her blink. 'I'm glad you like it. Do you think your guests will?'

His eyes shifted, roaming around the elegant proportions of the bedroom, lingering on the big bed.

'Yes. This should suit Ruth. She's used to only the best.'

The answer was revealing, Lacey thought as she drove back too late for the start of Mike's party. How naive of her ever to have thought that *she* might have influenced his moods. All his temper and tension were obviously caused by his desire to create something beautiful for Ruth. 'I've picked up the pieces once——' Don had said. Maybe after this visit, he would have to do it all over again.

The party was a haze of smoke and a bass blare of music when Lacey arrived. She kissed Mike, embraced a few mutual friends and fetched herself a drink which she consumed in double quick time. It failed to remove the sour taste in her mouth—the bitterness that came from having spent the past gruelling weeks planning and perfecting the rooms for the woman Luke loved. Ironic.

The second drink failed too, but the third and fourth did much better. Her head began to buzz pleasantly and her mouth smiled a lot.

'It really *was* a surprise!' Mike told her. 'When I came to the door and found the place tidy—*that* was a bigger surprise than this mob leaping out of the bedroom.'

Beth was beside him, looking like an advertisement for healthy living with her tan skin, pink cheeks and shining hair. Her slim, strong body was encased flatteringly in the straw-coloured taffeta and she rustled prettily every time she moved.

'I delayed as long as I could,' she said to Lacey, looking a little anxiously at her friend's odd happy/haunted expression.

'For a while I thought you'd set me up with Beth,'

Mike grinned. 'We sat on the sofa having drinks and making polite conversation for so long that I began to think I'd been roped into a blind date with her.'

'Then why didn't you leave?' Beth retorted, a trifle stiffly.

Mike looked her up and down. 'Because I'm *not* blind,' he said softly. 'Now come and rustle your taffeta at me.' He took her off among the crowd that bounced about in a cleared area of the living room and Lacey watched for a few moments, wondering muzzily if that brief matchmaking urge weeks ago had been so silly after all.

She danced herself once or twice and the fourth drink kept the smile on her mouth, if nowhere else. Mike asked her about the Harrow job, looking at her a bit oddly and she gaily assured him that their biggest client had been pleased with Stage One.

'Well,' she giggled. 'He said "You've done a fine job" so I think he was pleased.'

'Have you seen him play yet?' Beth wanted to know.

'Yes, I've seen him play.' Her head whirled a little and she felt her smile waver.

'Is he still good?'

'Oh yes. He's good. He plays like the devil himself.'

And she was back in the devil's court the following Tuesday, steeling herself to meet Gerard Harrow and the woman whose change of mind had so changed Luke. But the guests were not around, at least not where Lacey could see them. She heard the murmur of male voices once or twice—the medium pitch of a woman's laugh in a four-note scale—and that was enough to churn her stomach. There was a new tension about the lovely old house. Lacey could feel it in the air.

And when she saw Luke with the two newcomers, descending the broad stairs it was as if their ravelled emotions reached out and chilled her. Stupid, she told herself again. She was letting her imagination run away with her. Perhaps Ruth had made the right choice after all and loved Gerard—perhaps Gerard didn't care that Luke had been her first choice—perhaps Luke didn't really love her still . . . perhaps.

But their faces told another story. And the language of their bodies. Gerard, six years older than Luke, was more drawn than his photographs in her scrapbook but more distinguished, too, with the bearing of a man who knew his worth. There was about his eyes though as they rested on his brother and his wife, a look of regret or pain or both and his body was tense giving him a look of separateness from the other two. As if *they* were the pair and he the outsider.

Luke was smiling, the tight smile of a host under strain and his face was locked into the lines that made Lacey long to stroke them away. You fool, she said silently as she stood there riveted by the trio. He has women a-plenty to do that. Somehow she found it difficult to focus on the woman. Ruth Harrow. This woman had loved Luke and had his love in return then let it go. If the angle of her head, the wide concentration of her eyes was anything to go by, she could be having second thoughts. Ruth Harrow's attention was glued to Luke and though her well-tended hands twisted together, her four-note laugh rang out melodic into the high foyer. In her early thirties, she was a lovely woman. Lacey wished it was not so but she saw the smooth lines of her face, the slender, girlish body and the perfect grooming, and acknowledged her attraction. She was the girl in the funeral photograph. The girl with the frozen face. Somehow Lacey had built up a picture of a chill, unfeeling person who had thrown over Luke from ambition. Looking at her Lacey questioned Don's portrayal of her. There was feeling there and a warmth that showed even through her tension. Better for Luke, she thought, if she had been cold. Easier to forget.

Luke saw her halfway through something he was saying and stopped on the last stair. They came over and he made the introductions, his blue eyes looking her over impassively but missing nothing. She shook hands with Gerard and made bright small-talk to his wife and all the time felt Luke's eyes on her. Today she wore a cream skirt and jacket with a silk shirt patterned cream and pale emerald. Her hair was whirled into a knot and her glasses perched on her nose. With a stab of her forefinger she pushed them on more securely.

'The suite we are using is beautiful, Miss Teale,' Ruth Harrow smiled.

'Thank you, Mrs Harrow. Of course I merely interpreted Luke's ideas.'

There was a flicker of interest from both the Harrows when she used his first name.

'You're too modest, Lacey,' Luke put in with a mocking smile about his lips. 'You had quite a few ideas of your own that surprised me.'

So that was how it was going to be, she thought. And she had wasted her sympathy on him. Whatever Mr Luke Harrow had been through, she wasn't going to be his doormat—though she might be fool enough to want him, and though he might hold the second contract over her head like the sword of Damocles. Her smile was brilliant. Gerard Harrow blinked.

'Yes. Unfortunately first impressions often foster ideas that are better discarded. My later thoughts were far more constructive.'

She was pleased to see that Luke got the message. He wasn't about to use her as a dummy to assuage his frustration at having Ruth around and out of reach. A little more small talk and she escaped to the study where Gerard found her later as she slipped her things into her attaché case to leave.

'I'm just leaving, Mr Harrow, if you want to use the room.'

'No hurry, Miss Teale.' He went to look at the glass fronted bookshelves while she rolled up her drawings and snapped closed her case. He rattled the knob on the bookcase doors and she said helpfully, I believe the key is kept in the cupboard below it there.'

He grinned over his shoulder at her, 'No need for that.' With his shoulder against it, he hit his closed fist once further down the frame and the doors opened.

'Violà,' he made a Gallic gesture with his long, thin hands and smiled at her surprise. 'I grew up with the idiosyncracies of this bookcase, Miss Teale. My father kept all the forbidden books in it and the occasional wicked paperback in his top desk drawer——' he indicated the desk she had just cleared, '—Luke and I learned at an early age how to unlock the mysteries of literature you might say.'

She laughed, imagining two boys huddled over a forbidden book, looking up the naughty passages.

'He might have done it on purpose to encourage you to *want* to read. A bit of reverse psychology.'

His eyes, remarkably like Luke's, crinkled and his thin face was made almost handsome with his laughter.

'Do you know, that's often occurred to me since. If so, it worked. I'm a keen reader and so is Luke.' He lifted out a heavy old book as he spoke and closed the glass doors. 'This was the one I wanted. I wondered if it had survived two moves from our old house.'

Her lips twitched. 'Does it fall open at page 206?' she asked.

Gerard gave a shout of laughter. 'Not this one. *The Trade Routes of the East-India Company* wasn't one of the objects of our break-ins. But I can see that you might have read the odd novel undercover so to speak.'

'Yes. Only in my case I used to climb up into a tree with a paperback hidden inside my Maths text book. Of course I was sprung in the end. I asked for it—using a Maths book of all things was bound to invite suspicion, especially when it had me riveted for hours on end.'

They walked out into the passageway and Gerard's laugh echoed upwards again with hers. His earlier tension seemed to have subsided. What a very nice man he was, Lacey thought.

'Good night, Mr Harrow. Pleasant reading.'

'Call me Gerry, please.'

'Gerry then. Call me Lacey.'

He took her hand briefly. 'Goodnight, Lacey.'

He went up the staircase and Lacey turned smiling to the side entrance. Luke waited there, one hand on his hip, the other flat against the door—the way he'd stood that night at his hotel. The sound of their laughter would have carried to him here. But there was no echo of it on his face.

'Finished—so early?' he questioned as she drew close

and she almost said that she had a long drive back to Sydney before she remembered her fictional 'staying over'.

'Was there something else you wanted me to do, Luke?' she countered coolly and met the intense blue of his eyes with a little shock all over again. Shaking his head, he opened the door and followed her out into the late afternoon sun. Spring was lengthening into summer and the days were warmer and longer. There was a touch of new lime on Fremont's old trees, a tight-budded promise to the bare limbs of the jacaranda.

Underfoot the gravel was warm and their steps were noisy on it as they walked to her car. Her body zinged with Luke's closeness, its signals all mixed up as always when he was around. Why on earth was he following her?

'That was quick work,' he said as she opened her door. 'First names basis with Gerry already . . . and him so reserved too.' It was said with a sneer that annoyed her.

'I found your brother to be most pleasant.'

'Of course you did. It's Gerry's stock in trade to be pleasant.'

'Then he does it very well,' she said, wanting to ask him what his stock in trade was. But there was no point in prolonging any conversation with Luke. It would only rebound on her.

'Goodnight, Luke,' she pushed her glasses firmly on and started the motor. The car coughed and heaved a few times. Then it stopped. She repeated the procedure and the same thing happened.

'Put up the hood and I'll have a look at it,' Luke said briskly and she did as he bade, trying the starter once or twice at his command before he slammed the bonnet closed again.

'Is this the trouble you had with it before?' he asked and she nodded. 'Well,' he smiled mockingly, '—you've got it again.'

'Thanks, that's a big help. May I use your phone?'

'We'll ring a mechanic tomorrow. Come on. I'll drive you to your parents' place.'

Lacey chewed her lip. That was the problem. She was on her way back to Sydney, not to her parents, who weren't expecting her and had no free beds anyway now that her father's army pals were down from Orange.

'Well—come on.' Luke opened her door and held out a hand to her. She looked up at him, trying to gauge his reaction if she told him she'd lied to him. Eyes narrowed, he leaned into the car.

'Something on your mind, Lacey?'

This was ridiculous, she decided. She should have told Luke flatly from the start that she would prefer to travel hours every day than to stay overnight at Fremont. It was cowardly of her to have pretended the compromise of sleeping over at her parents' house.

'It's like this, Luke. I was intending to commute to and from Sydney this week. My parents have guests at present and no spare bed. In short——'

There was a silence.

'In short, you haven't a roof over your head tonight unless I drive you back to Sydney or invite you to stay here.' There was a smile on his face but she didn't like the look of it.

'And will you invite me to stay here tonight, Luke?'

'No.' He said it with quiet relish.

'All right, then,' she said levelly. 'Could I make a phone call to order a cab?'

He folded his arms and shook his head, smiling. 'It serves you right for lying to me,' he said as if she was a recalcitrant child. This, on top of his bad temper and moods and the unpalatable sight of him smiling on his sister-in-law was too much for Lacey.

'I see.' She got out of the car and slung her bag over her shoulder, leaving the attaché case on the car seat. 'Then I'll just have to find some alternative transport won't I? Until then, I'll walk,' she told him tersely.

'In those heels?' He looked at her stiletto-heeled beige sandals.

'That's right. Good night.' She set off down the drive, wobbling a bit on the gravel, then moved to walk on the grass which was only marginally better.

'Lacey——' he called in amused exasperation. It was

the softest tone she'd heard from him in weeks. Her eyes smarted at it. A stone turned her ankle and she righted herself before she could fall, and made her exit from the front gates.

A quick glance showed Luke still standing watching her, his hands on hips and a faint air of puzzlement about him. Had he expected her to come running back to him, begging accommodation for the night?

Girded by anger she hurried along the road outside Fremont's iron railings, covering a lot of ground before the edges roughened and her ankle really did give way, sending her hurtling forward. Luckily she broke her fall with her hands but sustained a few scratches even so and muttered angrily, placing the blame squarely where it belonged.

'You utter vengeful pig, Luke Harrow . . .'

She took off her shoes and with them dangling from her hand, strode out in her stockinged feet, moving further off the road as she heard the sound of an engine behind her.

The white Alfa Romeo slowed alongside. After a glance she ignored it. It stopped and the passenger door opened, but she strode on by it, too angry to see the sensible course of action. Her feet were hurting already as they contacted the tiny stones and bits of twig, and the road stretched out ahead of her unmarked by bus stops or phone booths as she knew all too well, for at least another mile.

'Lacey——' She didn't look back and two doors slammed in quick succession followed by the roar of the motor. Her heart began to thump faster at the angry sound and when the white car shot past her to the shade of a willow and the driver got out and waited for her, leaning against the passenger side, she stopped for a moment. It would be easy, comfortable to simply walk over and get in and be driven somewhere. Lacey's throat closed up suddenly in a rush of self-pity. Not just for this immediate plight but for the whole darned mess that she'd got herself into by falling in love with such a man as Luke. She admitted it at last. It wasn't going to wear off like infatuation. It was going to stay and stay and spoil her for any other man. Temper took over and she marched forward to the waiting man and as she reached the back of the car, dodged across the road and continued on the opposite grass verge.

'Lacey—don't be a fool——' he roared and she began to run as she heard his footsteps heavy and fast on the road. She had to run for the tears that she had denied were streaming now and there was no way she wanted Luke to see that. With one hand she dashed the moisture away. Her glasses became smudged and streaked so she took them off, folding them in one hand as she rushed along, conscious of Luke gaining on her. Another glance over her shoulder proved her downfall. Literally. She tripped and sprawled on to the tufting grass, rolled a little and lay still, all the breath squeezed from her.

'You stupid little——' Luke dropped to one knee beside her and when she opened her eyes and saw him leaning over her, she turned her head away to hide a new rush of tears.

'Are you hurt?' he snapped, and his hands touched her ankle, moved on up her legs to probe her ribs on to which she'd fallen. One had brushed her breast and the sensation shot fire through her, banishing the foolish weakness.

'Leave me alone. I'm all right. Don't maul me please.' She began to sit up.

'Maul you—why you——!' He jerked her upright so that her hair slipped finally from its pins, then stood up hauling her with him. The pain in one ankle shot up her leg but she shifted her weight and glared at him.

'You didn't have to come after me, Mr Harrow. Run on home to your guests. I can look after myself.'

'Like hell you can. Look at you.'

'If you imagine I'm about to plead with you to give me a lift or a "roof over my head" as you so quaintly put it, forget it. Did you think I'd give up after just half a lap of your driveway?'

Inexplicably his expression softened. 'To tell you the truth, I did, Lacey.'

'And then, if I'd been a good girl and prepared to pay the price, I would have been offered accommodation?'

The blue eyes darkened. He frowned. 'No—I——'

'You can wave all sorts of threats over my head, Luke—threaten to sue Mike and me, dangle contracts, use every mean little opportunity that comes your way, but you won't get me crawling to you——' she pushed away his supporting hand, '—and if I have to sleep outside under a w-willow, I'd rather do that than——' her voice wavered and she hitched her bag and stepped forward on to her sore ankle. It jarred right up to her hip and she made a small cry and crumpled. Luke caught her, lifted her feet from the ground to stare down at her pallor. Her wild words had only warded off the tears temporarily and now they poured down her face.

'Lacey—for God's sake—don't cry——'

She couldn't see him at all now but, as he began to walk on the road, clutched his shirt with one hand and her bag and shoes with the other. Then he bent with her and sat down in the passenger seat of the car, so that she was across his knees and crushed against him in the close confinement. He pulled a handkerchief from his pocket and wiped her face so that she could see him again. And that made it worse.

Through the car's open door came the dozy sounds of late afternoon—the far-off sound of a tractor, a magpie's call, the rustle of long grass and the willow tree that dropped its leafy skipping ropes to the windscreen. She looked into his face and was lost.

'Lacey,' he murmured and brushed away the last trace of moisture from her cheeks. 'What's happened to us . . .?' But she barely heard the words, for his hand slipped to her hair and his mouth was on hers and all she could think was that it had been too long and the days of seeing him and not touching were over at last. Her bag and shoes dropped from her hand and she put her arms about him, driving fingers into his hair, kneading the hard muscles of his back. Under the pressure of his kiss her mouth parted and with a deep intake of breath, Luke held her even closer, his lips and tongue exploring with a raw hunger. Then he eased her away again and ran a hand over her thigh, silk-smooth in sheer nylon where her skirt had ridden up, and over the jutting contour of her hip to her waist and the swell of her breast. Her shirt buttons yielded to his touch ... the front catch of her bra released and the lace and nylon parted. Luke slipped his hands under her arms and lifted her so that her face tilted forward over his thick, dark-blond hair that smelled of the day itself—grass and willows and summer coming—and his mouth found the nipple of one breast then the other inside the curtains of her unfastened shirt and jacket.

'Luke,' she whispered, putting his name to the coloured visions that exploded in her. I love you, Luke. Silently she told him, her hands loving him. He lowered her. Slowly. Lips caressing slopes and hollows, tender skin in shadow ... her hair, pale in filtered light. Lacey touched his face as he leaned over her, touched his parted lips and his breath was warm on her fingers. I love you, Luke. She slipped a hand to his neck and urged him to her kiss.

A car passed, a comet of sound in the gentle afternoon. Luke straightened, stared down at her where she lay in his arms. The noise of the vehicle came belatedly to Lacey, but gradually she took in the details she had forgotten—the roof of the car, the willow fronds draping the car's windows, the late daylight bright on her disarray. Luke's hand was shaped about her breast and she stayed there a moment longer savouring the sensation before reality rushed in.

'God, Lacey—I forgot where we were——' Luke breathed and held her close again. 'If it was dark, I'd take you out there on the grass and make love to you——' The words were mumbled against her forehead and his mouth lingered there a moment before he let her go and got out of the car. In the willow's shade he tucked in his shirt and ran a hand over his hair.

If it was dark—Lacey thought. If it was dark, she might have let him take her out there on the grass. Fool. And what would she be then? Another win for the champion. Maybe a little different from the others. But it was not much of a consolation to know that her only distinction might have been that he'd played his game with her outdoors. On a grass court, she thought with dismal humour. She fixed her clothes, hurrying through the undignified process, but Luke had the sensitivity to stay outside, leaning against the driver's door for a few minutes. When he got in, she administered one last tug to her skirt to bring it over her knees. Luke put his hand on hers, finding her palm with his thumb and even this small touch after so much else, rushed along her nerves. At last she looked at him. There was elation, desire in his eyes—the bitterness had lifted from his face, blotted away and replaced with supreme confidence and maybe triumph.

'Let's go home,' he said in a voice still husky and the promise in the words was clear. Home—where Ruth was already paired off with his brother. Home—to the guest room with the curtained bed and the cushions. A late night knock on the door—and then another conquest for him. For a few minutes she was tempted to let it all happen. He might even love her in his way for a month or two, a year. But as a 'dose of the poison'. As an antidote to Ruth.

'It might be better if I returned to the city, Luke. I don't have any spare clothes.'

It was like watching a curtain come down. His eyes cleared of passion and his facial lines settled into the bleak pattern that tore at her.

'Playing the tease again, Lacey?'

'No. Luke—I'm sorry. I shouldn't have let you——'

'Let *me*!' he sneered. 'You weren't exactly playing dead. In fact the driver of that car could be excused for thinking I was being seduced.'

Her face flamed. 'I over-reacted, I was upset. Can we forget it please, Luke?'

'I'm sure *you* will. You seem prone to' forgetting things—your partner, for instance.' He started the car. 'You no doubt keep a few spare clothes at your parents' place?' he said tautly over the sports car's hum.

'Well, yes, but——'

'Then we'll pick them up and bring them if clothes are your only objection. I've decided to offer you a bed for the night, Lacey.' The car screeched out on to the road. 'And a key for your door. . . .'

Refusal was the sensible course, but Lacey couldn't bring herself to make it. With him looking hard as granite, it would be inviting ridicule to say that she was afraid he would press his attentions on her. A bubble of laughter, hysterical almost, lurked in her throat. 'Press his attentions'—what a bygone terms to use with her skin afire even now from his touch. More Gothic ramblings.

'All right. Thank you.'

She gave him directions, hoping that her gadabout parents and their guests were out. Not that it could matter all that much she supposed, if he found out from them that she had been his ardent fan. But a small part of her curled up at the idea of him knowing.

'Can you walk?' he asked when they pulled up and she nodded.

The cottage was quiet, nestled in her mother's wild garden. Lacey used her key and Luke followed her, hands sunk in pockets, face sunk in brooding thought.

'You're lucky to have grown up here,' he said unexpectedly.

'Why do you say that?'

'The place has a—good feeling.' He looked in at the living room with its old oak china cabinet, her mother's tapestry cushions and the clutter of her father's papers and magazines.

'Yes, it does,' she agreed and stopped nervously at the door of her old bedroom. Luke was right behind her.

'Don't look so anxious. I won't throw you down on your schoolgirl's bed. In fact, if I come in I'll want your promise not to ravish *me* after that eager performance of yours.'

She went in then, red-faced, limping a bit, and tried to ignore him as he looked around the room that had been hers all her childhood days and some of her grown days too. His gaze drifted unknowing over the wardrobe where she had pinned his picture behind her clothes.

'Hmmph,' he grunted. 'It needs something.' He turned unreadable blue eyes on her. 'Dandelions, maybe?' he said, and walked into the hall and towards the back of the house. Lacey opened a drawer and found some underwear and spare tights and an amber dress that she had left there last week. They were all neatly segregated from Archie's thick socks and twill shirts. Luke was standing at a window overlooking the back yard when she went to find him.

'Which is the tree that you climbed with your forbidden books?' he enquired, half-turning when she came back.

'You were listening.'

'Your voices carried.'

'That one,' she pointed out the quince tree before she thought. It was the one in the photograph. Not that he would know. If he had ever seen that silly little tribute from a fan, he wouldn't remember it. 'It's a quince tree.'

'Quite a distinctive shape,' he said thoughtfully and her heart boomed. 'We had one like that when I was a kid. On the property we used to have before the——' he stopped and frowned at the tree.

'They've gone out of fashion,' she elaborated and went on a bit about the distinctive flavour of the fruit. 'Ours hasn't set fruit for years now. At one time quince trees were a must in every garden. A lot of the old houses around here have one still. That one's probably fifty years old.'

He faced her, his sardonic smile acknowledging the nervousness that set her rambling about quince trees. But he couldn't know that her nerves were edgy for reasons other than that scene on the road.

They walked through to the hallway again and were halted by a high, wavering voice.

'Just stay right where you are or you'll be sorry,' Janet Teale peeped out of the living-room doorway, a garden spade raised in her hands. 'Oh—Lacey——' she gasped, lowering it. 'You gave me a terrible shock. When I came home and found the front door ajar I thought we had burglars . . .' she saw Luke and stopped, her mouth open. 'Aren't you——?' Luke

Harrow. How do you do.' She swapped the spade to her left hand and held out her right. 'I'm Lacey's mother.'

Luke smiled, one eye on the spade.

'You equip yourself well for burglars, Mrs Teale.'

She laughed. 'Well I wasn't sure if that sports car out the front had anything to do with it, but I thought if it did, then I had a very successful burglar on my hands, so I wasn't taking any chances. Gray isn't going to believe me when I tell him I nearly hit a Wimbledon hero on the head with a spade.'

'I'm already a fallen hero anyway,' he said dryly.

Janet Teale smiled up at him. 'No. You just didn't give everyone time to wake up to that rubbish in the press, that's all.'

'You think I threw in the towel too soon?'

'Much too soon. You had fans who never doubted you for a minute, I can tell you.' Lacey winced, but her mother's eyes didn't so much as stray in her direction. 'But of course, it's easy for me to tell you you should have hung on. And a bit selfish too. Gray and I would have liked to see an Aussie keep that Wimbledon title for a few years.'

'I might not have kept it, Mrs Teale,' he said with a quirk of one eyebrow. 'There was some fine competition around at the time.'

She gave a snort of dismissal to that. 'You would have kept it. Now—what's up? Where is your car, Lacey?'

Lacey explained that due to car trouble she had to stay over at Fremont, and if her mother noticed a certain crumpling of her clothes and the odd grass stain from her flight, she made no comment.

'Gray will be sorry to have missed this. He's taken a few days off from the shop and is out fishing with Archie and Monty. They promised me a bucket of fish for dinner but I came home to put a roast on, just in case,' she laughed. 'I'd ask you to stay for coffee but I have to change for my Aikido class.'

'Aikido?' Lacey repeated, 'Weren't you doing jazz ballet?'

'I was, but oh—everyone does that, don't they? Sorry about the rush. It's a pleasure to meet you, Mr Harrow.'

'Luke,' he said.

'Luke, then. It's wonderful to know that you are restoring The Big House. Lacey has been in love with it since she was a little girl. . . .'

In a rush of energy, she was gone to change. They went out. Luke took the spade from its incongruous position in the polished hall and left it outside. As he stood it against the brick house wall, he looked at Lacey.

'Like mother—like daughter. Only you don't need a spade.'

CHAPTER EIGHT

BUT it was only his ego that had been dealt a blow, Lacey concluded that evening. As confirmation she was presented with the picture of Luke and Ruth, mere inches apart, gazing into each others eyes. Her hand lay along his arm. His hand touched her waist. They were in the small sitting room upstairs—one Lacey had admired with its late-Victorian addition of ornate timber fretwork curved into the wide, arched entrance. Ruth and Luke were framed in it. Lovers in a valentine. And Lacey hurried away as fast as her tender ankle would let her, her feet noiseless on the lush, new carpet, with that one quick image of them imprinted in her mind.

As she went, the scene went on unrolling ... Luke would be bending his head, kissing her ... for it was obvious that they were two people on the brink of a kiss.

She dressed for dinner in the low-necked amber dress. Somehow she had to hide her hurt away. And her distaste. Luke had held her in his arms earlier this evening and but for the circumstances, would have taken his lovemaking to conclusion. And now, hours later, he held the woman who was married to his brother. And somewhere on the fringes of all this activity was the attractive Leonie Stewart, ready no doubt to soothe him when he had a spare minute or two. 'He tells them whatever is necessary ...' his mother had said, and she recalled the pure craftsmanship of the words Luke had used to her. 'As for love, I'm not sure I know what that is anymore—you remind me of better days when I did know——'

'Oh boy,' she muttered and walked about the bedroom, testing her ankle which was almost normal again. He used his bitter past like some men used war wounds. Hinted at a capacity for love that was lost—

and women couldn't resist thinking *they* would be the one to restore his capacity. Except Ruth Harrow. She *knew* she was the only one who could.

Lacey brushed her hair loose, glared at herself in the mirror then put up a hand from habit to push her glasses on to her nose and realised foolishly that they weren't there. She looked in her handbag and closed it again, remembering that she'd cried all over them, taken them off while Luke chased her. Had she had any close work to do, she would have noticed sooner.

'You dropped them, you idiot,' she said aloud. They were there in the long grass across the road from the willow tree. Her green eyes looked back from the mirror, wide, angry and hurt. Wearing her glasses wouldn't change any of that, but might have provided some camouflage. She went down to dinner feeling somehow naked.

Lacey had never expected to sit at the lovely old cedar dining table beneath the gasolier that she had found for Luke and, in the circumstances, she didn't want to. But dinner was more pleasant than she anticipated. Mainly because of Paula Harrow and Gerry, who between them kept a steady conversation flowing. Paula, looking well and happier than Lacey had seen her, directed most of her attention towards Gerry who skilfully deflected it to someone else. Luke spoke to his mother once or twice and Lacey noticed that she barely acknowledged him. Ruth, on the other hand, almost ignored everyone else but Luke, and Lacey felt a rush of sympathy for her husband whose excellent manners held a touch of anxiety.

'I see your ankle is giving no more trouble,' Luke said in a gap in the conversation. Everyone's attention turned to her and Lacey knew he'd done it deliberately. The others had shown some surprise at her re-appearance. Car trouble seemed a lame reason to be here for the night. Gerry's polite follow up to Luke's question forced Lacey to fabricate a story about falling on the gravel drive and a glance at the table's head showed her that the host was deriving some pleasure from it.

'No glasses tonight, Lacey?' he commented as soon as she'd finished explaining away her sore ankle. She held his eyes for a moment. It was probably the first time he'd seen her so long without them—except for moments of anger and when he'd removed them himself. Her face heated.

'I—seem to have misplaced them,' she said and his eyes narrowed as if he might have recalled how and where she could have done so. But he said nothing else.

'What is the matter with your car, Lacey?' Gerry asked her and she resigned herself to providing the bulk of the conversation and told him.

'I'll have a look at it in the morning if you like,' he offered with a smile. Lacey looked at his well-tended, pale hands and tried to imagine Gerry's immaculate figure bending over her car engine.

'Come off it, Gerry,' Luke cut in. 'You've been chauffeur-driven the last eight years. You wouldn't know what the motor of a car looked like.'

Gerry ignored the trace of sarcasm. 'It's like riding a bike. You don't forget. Who—I ask you—got your first car going for you?'

'My first——?' Luke seemed startled. Enough to stop frowning.

'That damned awful beat-up old Holden of yours. Don't you remember? Long before you made yourself rich from prizemoney. Pink it was,' he said to Lacey, 'With a silver stripe along the sides . . . a foxtail and a skeleton dangling from the mirror. . . .'

'I did respray her,' Luke grinned, with a surprised look of reminiscence.

'Mm, you did. Metallic blue with a *red* stripe down the sides.'

'Oh yes——' Paula Harrow laughed and put a hand on Luke's sleeve, '—you worked so hard on that old car, Luke. You used to be covered in grease and oil. I remember your father saying. . . .' She stopped suddenly, a puzzled look on her face as she looked at him. Then she took her hand from Luke and put it to her head. 'Will you excuse me—I have the most dreadful headache.'

Luke went with her and after a moment Ruth
followed. The dining room remained silent after they
had gone and eventually Gerry said in explanation, 'I'm
afraid my mother hasn't been the same since the
accident.' Then he added, 'None of us have.'

She murmured something which prompted Gerry to
go on.

'Sorry, Lacey—I assume you know there was an
accident some years ago?'

'Yes, I knew.'

'It was hardest on Luke,' he turned his wineglass in
his hand, studying the contents that glowed ruby, 'I
should never have let him . . .' he seemed to remember
where he was and smiled at her. 'But we mustn't rake
out the family skeletons. Tell me, did you design this
interior too?'

She smiled and talked about her work and the house
with just a third of her mind. Another third was
wondering just what skeletons might be in the Harrow
closets. And the last was upstairs. Viewing another
valentine.

When Ruth came back she was laughing. So was
Luke. Lacey raised her hand to adjust her glasses and
found nothing there. It was a lost feeling. Gerry
fidgeted with his napkin, pleating and smoothing the
edge of it absently, and she felt a stab of sympathy for
him. He must have known that his brother was Ruth's
first choice. Anger dragged her eyes from the two. She
drank her wine rather fast and after a few minutes
Gerry refilled her glass.

'Do you often live in on assignments?' Ruth enquired
as they ate dessert. Lacey had to admit that she was
friendly enough. She would have liked to dislike her on
grounds other than that she had Luke's love.

'Rarely,' she said brightly. 'But then most of my jobs
are in or close to the city. I have stayed over once or
twice when the work has been distant. But I try to avoid
it. My partner doesn't like me to be away too much.'

She caught Luke's eye and as his lip curled her hand
went automatically to the glasses that weren't there. No
lenses to hide behind tonight.

'Understandable,' Gerry said, looking from her to his brother and back again. 'She'd have two jobs to do.'

'My partner is a man,' she explained without looking at the head of the table, 'and his reasons for not wanting me to be away are both business and personal.'

'Oh. Oh I see.' Gerry flicked a glance at Luke.

'Yes—my mother calls it a "modern arrangement". But who knows, one day we might go all conventional and buy a ring.' She calmly went on eating, marvelling at how easy it was to make herself Mike's mistress.

'I thought you were sharing with your friend, Beth?' Luke said in a harsh tone and this time she looked at him. It was easier now with something to bolster her.

'So I was. But she knew we'd eventually go our separate ways. We had a party on Friday night to celebrate. . . .'

He didn't like that. On Friday she'd been anxious to leave so that she could go to Mike's party. A little bit of truth she thought, could give such weight to a lie. Luke's mouth arranged itself into a straight line. He was forced to acknowledge that he was in the company of maybe the only two fish who'd got away. Herself because of a lucky accident and Ruth from choice. Although she might be prepared to let him try his line again.

The coffee was served in the lounge by Mrs Simmons and it seemed inevitable that Lacey should find herself with Gerry. The brief camaraderie between the brothers appeared to have gone. Luke sat apart with Ruth.

'My book *did* fall open,' Gerry said after a time. 'But at page 190.'

'Heavens—don't tell me *The Trade Routes of the East India Company* had a saucy bit?'

His quick laugh drew Luke's gaze momentarily. 'No saucy bits. But I found an old love letter from a girlfriend. Brenda Parks her name was,' he said reminiscently. 'A goddess—a veritable Juno.'

'A goddess called Brenda Parks?' she giggled.

'Ah yes. She was rather thin about the legs as I recall, and freckled. Red hair . . .'

Lacey laughed again at his expression.

'. . . but it was her endowment in—er—other areas that earned her the title of goddess.' He grinned at her reaction.

'At fourteen I had very obvious priorities. What was *your* idea of a pin-up as a teenager, Lacey?'

Involuntarily her eyes went to Luke and she covered up with a laughing account of the boy next door. Gerry went along with it but there was a curious look in his eyes that made her doubt that she'd been quick enough with her camouflage.

'Come—show me the changes you're going to wreak in the ballroom, Lacey,' he said later when they were talking about her work; on the way he stopped at the drinks cabinet and filled two glasses of wine to take with them. 'One must view a ballroom with the correct accessories,' he told her solemnly and it occurred to Lacey that Gerry might be just the tiniest bit tiddly. The effect of her own hastily consumed wine lingered, but Gerry had taken several scotches since his coffee.

'I'm not going to *wreak* any changes,' she objected belatedly as he flung open the panelled double doors to the big, empty room with its windowed, arched orchestra alcove. Moonlight tossed the pallid outline of the uncovered window across a discarded chaise longue and spilled over on to the floor. 'Wreak—that makes me sound like a demolitionist!'

He laughed raised his glass to her, then drank. 'Let's put these down, m'dear, I hear the musicians playing our song.'

He set the glasses on the floor and whisked her into his arms. They waltzed around the huge room and for a few moments Lacey could almost imagine the palms and the orchestra and the rustling dresses of the ladies. But it was only a momentary haunting. Gerry began to hum a waltz and the uneven sound of it made her laugh again. Two refugees, she thought—from reality. He whirled her faster and she became pleasantly dizzy.

'You're fantastic at this, Gerry,' she gasped.

'I should be. I've pushed enough diamond-studded ladies about in diplomatic circles.'

He hummed the Straus waltz again and she joined

him, their voices rising eerily in the empty room as they circled one last time and stopped. Gerry pulled her close for a second and she leaned her giddy head on his shoulder.

'You waltz divinely, m'dear.'

'Thank you, sir. I haven't had so much fun since I burned down the chicken coop when I was eleven. . . .'

He laughed. 'No! Did you?'

A sound from the doorway turned their heads. Standing in the shaft of light from the corridor was Luke, his feet apart and arms folded as if he might have been there for some time.

'It's the chaperone,' murmured Gerry and Lacey giggled as he let her go, even as she felt the cold draft of Luke's presence. But Gerry retained her hand, bent to put his lips briefly to it in a courtly old-world gesture.

'Ruth wants you,' Luke told his brother in crisp tones.

'Well, doesn't that make a change?' Gerry said. His shoes made echoing sounds as he went to the door.

'Don't be a fool, Gerry.'

The older man's voice was suddenly sober. 'No. Of course not.' He paused, put his hand on Luke's shoulder for a moment. 'Goodnight, Luke. 'Night, Lacey,' he called back. Her name hung in the ballroom's empty grandeur after he had gone.

She stood for a few moments in the room's dusk where neither moonlight nor man-light reached and the race of her heart beat was not from her waltz with Gerry.

'I must go too——' she began, but as she took a step forward so did Luke and she stopped as he blocked her way.

'What a little bitch you are,' he said, scarcely above a whisper and the words bit into the emptiness. 'Do you just automatically have to ensnare every man you meet?'

'I don't know what you're talking about, Luke. I'm going to bed.' Boldly she detoured around him, looking ahead to the rhomboid of hall light as sanctuary. Her foot touched the empty wine glasses and they toppled with a small sound of glass breaking. One rolled back and forth as Lacey recovered and made for the door. Luke spun, grabbed her wrist and yanked on it, then let her go, forcing her to take several stumbling small steps into the centre of the room to save herself from falling.

'What a performance,' he sneered. 'Why, I doubt Gerry has had such a professional going over for years. The poor guy is probably upstairs wondering how soon he can knock on your door. Will *he* get the cold shoulder, Lacey, m'dear?' he mimicked Gerry. 'Will you tell *him* you've changed your mind?'

There was a cold glitter in his eyes and Lacey backed away. He came after her until he, too, was in the dimness, away from the two patches of light through which she and Gerry had danced.

'What are you inferring? I hardly know your brother,' she said stiffly and he laughed. It was a scratchy sound. Mirthless.

'Inferring, the lady says! You should be an actress Lacey. You make outraged virtue look almost genuine.' Even in the grey velvet darkness she saw his eyes rake her from head to foot. 'You hardly knew *me* either, did you? Forgotten your partner again—forgotten poor old Mike? Out of sight, out of mind. For a while there I thought it was only me who could make you forget him . . . but it's any man, isn't it, Lacey?' His contemptuous tone cut through the last delicate layer of insulation that the wine and Gerry's warmth had given her. 'I don't intend to listen to this, Luke.'

He seized her before she'd managed a step, hauled her close so that her head was forced back.

'You'll listen. You've forgotten something else tonight, Lacey. Gerry is married. Or don't your morals recognise that as a deterrent?'

'Yes, he's married,' her temper exploded at his hypocrisy, and she practically hissed the words at him. 'And I can see why it's him who is married and not you.'

'What do you mean?' Luke's voice came rough as sandpaper through his throat.

'Ruth made the right choice and if she's got any sense she'll stick by it.'

His fingers bit into her shoulders until Lacey winced.

'Yes, she preferred him. Has he been boasting about it, Lacey? How he cut in while I was occupied with—other things? He has such a smooth style, such panache, such an unblemished past has my brother. Do you prefer him too, Lacy?'

'Yes I do,' she flung at him and tried to wrench free of his hold. 'He's civilised and pleasant. It makes a change from your rotten temper and black moods and—and barely disguised blackmail to get what you want——'

'And he makes a change from your curly headed lover I suppose. So soon after you've moved in with him too,' he ground out.

'Let me go, Luke. You're a fine one to chide me about morals. You play your games with any partners you fancy, married or not. But don't credit others with your own lack of integrity. Gerry has my sympathy, with you doing your best to come between him and his wife——' The words ended in a gasp as he shook her hard and she felt his fury flood through her.

'Your sympathy is all he'll get, Lacey——' His arms snapped around her, dragging her against him. 'If anyone joins you on your bed tonight, it will be me.'

'You contemptible——' she hit out at him, followed up and hit him again, then as his grip loosened, rushed blindly away from him. But she chose the wrong patch of light and in the few seconds it took for her to realise her mistake, Luke had her cordoned off in the arched musician's alcove where the moonlight streamed through the bare window. Her back was against the glass, her arms braced each side of her on the frame and Lacey saw her shadow stretched out to Luke's feet.

'If you come near me, Luke, I warn you——' she began, her body trembling, but he paced forward until her shadow fell crookedly across him and she caught the expression that the moonlight found in his eyes. That was gone in an instant, for he pinioned her outflung wrists and bent his head so that she had no light at all. Just darkness and Luke, his temper venting itself on her, flaying her with a kiss as rough and cruel as those first ones had been, miracles of sensuality. She pressed back into the depth of the window but he released one of her hands and held her head so that she was joined to him at this one point, her lips crushed under his. Lacey pelted blows on his shoulder until he let her other hand free, but it was worse, much worse. For he hauled her body to his and her resistance began to die the moment she was denied the sanity of distance. With conscious effort she renewed her struggle. Luke, if he recognised her weakness, made no allowances for it. His hand clenched in her hair, pulled her head back and his lips travelled along the column of her neck. Tears sprang to her eyes as her scalp hurt but Luke pressed hard, ruthless kisses to her skin, lowering his head to the deep vee of her dress until his mouth reached the valley of her breasts at the fabric's barrier. Once more she tried to escape as he released one iron grip to pull down her zip. But his other hand dragged on her hair and though she flailed, he pushed the dress over one shoulder, then the other, and her struggles merely accelerated his intention as the garment slipped lower until it fell from her hips and to the floor.

'Luke—no——' she croaked through a throat constricted by its unnatural position, as her bra followed the dress to the floor and his hand spread over her buttocks, forcing her hard against him. At last the punishing hold on her hair eased. Instead Luke gripped her about the waist and spun her almost off her feet. Her calves hit something before she sprawled on the old chaise longue with its torn upholstery, and the moonlight flooded over her before Luke's shadow blotted it out. His weight pinned her, her legs outspread and her breath coming in ragged gusts.

Head raised, he looked down at her and her breathing slowed as he remained still. There would be no escaping him now she knew. For now her body was aiding him, making escape nigh impossible to attempt. Her bare skin was afire with the bunched muscle and sinew that pressed to hers; her body caught and held beneath him in its most vulnerable pose, could not fail to register that Luke wanted her badly.

'I was wrong,' he said very softly and her heart leaped in relief. He realised his mistake . . . it could not be like this, in anger, for them. . . .

'We don't need a bed. This time I won't let you go upstairs first.'

And though her mind and heart cried out at that, she forgot it as he touched her breasts and found the nipples with his tongue. She forgot that and everything else as Luke smoothed and kneaded and stroked until her head whirled under the bombardment of sensation. His hair was crisp to her touch, his shoulders hard and inexplicably suddenly bare beneath her fingers. The moonlight swam around them, a pale, sweet glow that silvered his face and body as he turned slightly in her arms. There was the rustle of clothing, then the whisper of his hands on her thighs and forgetfulness was complete in the fire of it as he stripped away the last of her coverings. Lacey wrapped her arms around him, binding him to her in an agony of anticipation. I love you, Luke, she said in her mind to drive away the memory that would rush back at this moment. This time she would not be reminded of those things that had denied him to her before—this time she would love him, even if he didn't know . . . I love you, Luke. 'Luke . . . yes. . . .'

The noises in the hall were alien, part of some other world. But the voice intruded.

'Mr Harrow—are you there?' Mrs Simmons called and Lacey heard the woman take a step into the room. Luke raised his head and his eyes glittered at Lacey.

'Yes, Mrs Simmons. No—don't bother with the lights please. What is it?'

'Your mother would like to see you if you're free,' the woman's voice sounded dubious, as if she guessed he might not be 'free' and Lacey made a panicky move even though she knew they could not be seen behind the arched wall from the doorway. Luke held her there, their bodies so nearly joined while this prosaic conversation went on. A hysterical laugh welled deep inside her—and a cry. His voice vibrated through her.

'Fine. I'll be with her in a few minutes. Go up and tell her, will you please?'

The woman's footsteps faded along the hall and Luke stood up. He looked down at Lacey's nakedness, then picked up her clothes and dropped them over her.

'Poor old Mike,' he said softly and began to dress. Silently she did the same, reaching for her zip with as much success as she reached for her reason. Luke turned her around, fastened it with a precise movement. His hands remained on her shoulders.

'If you want to finish this, Lacey, my willing little decorator, you can knock on *my* door.'

She sat down on the edge of the chaise longue because her knees suddenly buckled. He stopped in the archway to look back at her but the moonlight fell short and she couldn't see his face. Long after he had reached the hallway and his retreat was muffled on the carpet, she sat there—and remembered all that she had forgotten. Again.

Morning came, bright and impersonal, bringing unsuitable sunshine and cloudless skies as a sort of mockery to the rainy climate of her mind. What now would happen to the second Harrow contract she could only guess. Should Luke decide to leave it in the hands of Logan and Teale, she would have to find a way to cope with it for Mike's sake. And if he withdrew it? She stared out on to dewy, green lawns and hoped he would. To keep on seeing him was a reminder of his duality—what she had thought to be and what she knew him to be.

The wish to stay closeted away was strong, but Lacey dressed in yesterday's suit. Her flight and his pursuit had been sponged and pressed from it before the greater debâcle of last night. Resolutely she applied make-up and cinched back her hair. Again she pushed at her glasses with the gesture of long habit and again remembered that they were gone. She would have to drive along the road in search of them as soon as her car was fixed.

Gratefully Lacey snatched at the practicalities. First she had to phone a mechanic—phone Beth to set her mind at rest, something she should have done last night—find her glasses.

And speak to Luke. Find out what he intended about

the remainder of the work—and if she was to continue
the agony of coming here. Her heart bumped painfully
at the thought of seeing him again. She went down
early, too early to see anyone else for breakfast and had
a cup of coffee and some toast in the big, old kitchen.
Mrs Simmons eyed her with a curious expression once
or twice and Lacey thought again that the housekeeper
might have known that Luke was not alone in the
darkened ballroom last night. Maybe she had found the
broken remains of two wine glasses and drawn her
conclusions. She should care about that, she supposed.
In a day or two she might. In the study she used the
phone to contact a mechanic, spoke to Beth who was
breathlessly running late for work as usual. She sat
there at Luke's desk blankly when she'd hung up.

When the door opened in a taut arc minutes later, she
was still there, her hand on the phone, her eyes faraway
and bruised. There was a change in him. Something was
different, but she couldn't pinpoint it. But whatever it
was, it had nothing to do with her. For her the blue
eyes were shuttered, his mouth hard. Looking at her
hand on the phone he said, 'You finally remembered to
phone your flatmate I see.'

'Yes,' she admitted truthfully, though of course he
meant Mike.

'You really will have to be less—forgetful, Lacey,' he
said with that cynic's curl to his mouth.

'Luke——' she raised her chin proudly and met his
eyes. 'What do you want me to do about the work
here?'

After a few seconds he thrust his hands into his
pockets. 'Why, do it, Lacey. That's all.'

'You mean you want me to go ahead and handle the
job even after——?'

He strolled forward until his thighs touched the desk
edge. 'Why not? You've got class as a decorator if not
in anything else.' She flinched at the deliberate insult
and he stopped. 'However, I feel I can dispense with
your supervisory skills while I have guests. Next week
they will leave for Canberra and I'll be going to my
New England ranch. Come back then.'

'Very well. Do you want me to leave as soon as my car is fixed today?'

'Just as soon as you can, Lacey. And—keep away from Gerry, there's a good girl. Perhaps you could make do with one of the workmen for a few hours?'

The whitening of her face seemed to satisfy him. But she denied him any further satisfaction.

'With your permission, before I go I'll conduct another search for those paintings that have been mislaid.'

He nodded and she got up and went out, amazed at how evenly she walked when her body shook uncontrollably on the inside.

Her search for the paintings was fruitless. The storeroom and the beneath-stairs storage bore no trace and Mrs Simmons claimed no knowledge of them. Gerry appeared and spoke to her briefly, then went out. She didn't see Ruth but passed the housekeeper as she carried a breakfast tray upstairs. Later a mechanic turned up and gave her good news and bad about her car. It could be ready to drive again within two hours but it would cost a small fortune. He apologised profusely about the cost, blaming the price of steel, the unions, and the boss' overheads but Lacey would have paid double right then to be able to drive away from Fremont. While he worked on her car Lacey went to brief the men who had arrived to work on the downstairs sitting room. There were two of them—one young and muscular, the other middle-aged and loudly humorous. Low though she felt, she laughed at an outrageous witticism of the older man and as she withdrew from the room through the door held open for her by his athletic side-kick, Luke saw her.

'Taking my advice, Lacey?' he sneered as he eyed the grinning young man.

'Of course, Luke,' she said coolly. 'I have at least *two* hours to kill, or so the mechanic tells me.'

He had the grace to look discomfited, started to say something else. She never knew if it was an apology for he changed his mind and left her to stride away towards the sound of a four-note laugh.

It was in one of the two empty bedrooms upstairs that Lacey found the paintings. Unopened, they had been stored there, possibly by some well-meaning contractor, and a tarpaulin flung across them. They certainly hadn't been here on Friday, more's the pity, she thought and pulled the canvas away to unwrap them. But it was the plethora of frames and posters behind them that took her attention. Here were blown up photographs of Luke at his youthful best—photographs that might once have hung in his proud parents' house. There were a couple of paintings too, unremarkable except for the charred frames and Lacey carefully spread them out to look at them. They looked as if they had been in a fire. Behind more tennis pictures were family portraits in dimpled gold frames. A studio photo of Gerry and Luke in short pants with slicked back hair. Luke's boy's smile was gappy where his second teeth were halfway down. There was another of Paula Harrow, young and pretty, wearing an evening gown with her hands clasped in her lap. And one of Luke—she looked again, for the glass was broken and the frame blackened—no. It was his father. So like at first glance but for the darker hair.

'Miss Teale——' Lacey spun around, the picture of Luke Senior in her hand and found Paula Harrow behind her. 'Were you looking for something?'

She explained, indicated the paintings partly unwrapped and the woman smiled. 'Do you know, I think I like the replacements you hung better than these. In fact, I'd like one of them in my sitting room if that's possible.' She blinked a bit at the charred frame in Lacey's hands.

'Were these damaged in a fire, Mrs Harrow?'

Even as she asked, she remembered the fire in the entrance hall. Luke had mentioned that some damage was done to personal effects.

'Yes. Unfortunately before they were even unpacked. We don't know just what started it. . . .' Paula took the photo from Lacey and rubbed a finger over the sooty glass.

'It's a good portrait,' Lacey said for want of anything else.

'Yes it is. He's very photogenic.' She put it down and looked through the other pictures. 'Ah, this is the one.' She showed Lacey a photograph of a boyish Gerry on a horse. 'I thought Ruth might like to have this.'

Lacey wondered at the odd tingling down her spine as she finished unwrapping the paintings after Paula Harrow left. She leaned them against the wall and went to the door, looking back at the blackened portrait of Luke Harrow, Sr. It must have been a slip of the tongue. '—*is* photogenic' Paula Harrow had said. Is?

It was unfortunate that the motor mechanic stopped for a tea-break. For it meant that Lacey was still at Fremont when a snappy little hatchback drove up the gravel drive and discharged a slender, attractive woman in red who hurried smiling down to the courts where Luke was playing the machine again.

Lacey watched the woman raise her hand and give him a wave of greeting and felt at once bitchily jealous and deeply sorry for her.

'Just another notch on his racquet handle,' she muttered outside the coach-house and started when Don spoke at her elbow.

'What's that, Lacey?'

'Oh, Don. I just came to say goodbye. My car is nearly ready and I have to go. It will be next week when I come back and I thought you might be going to the other ranch with Luke.'

'Yes that's right.' He crinkled his eyes at her. 'What's the rush? I thought you were here until tomorrow.'

'Something's come up. My partner needs me.' Her eyes followed the splash of scarlet down to the courts and watched as the white-garbed man joined her.

'Oh yeah. Hmmm, weather's taken a turn for the worse.' She looked sharply at him. The sun was blazing down on them. 'Her name's Leonie. Leonie Stewart.' he added laconically.

'I know. *Mrs* Stewart,' she said in a tart tone. 'It's a good thing I'm leaving. Luke looks like starting a harem.'

'Ah no,' he shook his head, 'Don't go getting him mixed up with the other Luke. Now *he* was a collector.'

Don said wryly. She didn't register it for a minute maybe, then dragged her eyes from the couple talking near the courts.

'The other Luke? You mean his father was a womaniser, too?'

Don narrowed his eyes. 'I don't know where you get the idea that *my* boy is a womaniser. Luke's no monk, but he cares. Not like the old man. He was a fair bug—sorry, a devil he was where women were concerned. Love 'em and leave 'em that was his motto.' His face lengthened. 'Gave Paula one hell of a time. It was no wonder she——'

An awful dryness took Lacey by the throat. '—mixed up with the *other* Luke——' His words rang like a bell in her mind. '—where women are concerned he's a devil' Paula Harrow had said to her that night.

'. . . was popular all right with everyone. On the tennis circuit he was everyone's pal. Never played up with the women in the public eye—the girl players I mean. Luke kept him on the straight and narrow there . . . covered for him a few times. Poor bloody kid is still covering for him in a funny sort of way. . . .'

Paula Harrow's voice was clear in Lacey's head. 'He's photogenic—he's very photogenic——'

'—the boys were more mature than their father by the time they were fifteen I reckon . . . .'

Lacey grabbed his arm. 'He was right-handed wasn't he?'

Don stared. 'Who?'

'Luke's father.'

'Yeah, but why would you want to know that?'

Her throat was parched, painful and she swallowed once or twice. Don took a hold on her arms and looked into her face. 'What's the matter, Lacey?'

'The desk in the study was Luke's father's wasn't it? Gerry said so . . . I told Paula that we were replacing it with an antique piece made for a left-handed owner. She said "Luke's not left handed——"'

'She would've been thinking of his father——' he began.

'In the present tense?' She clutched at his forearms.

'Just this morning she looked at a photograph of her husband and said "He's very photogenic".' And the look on her face that day when she'd seen Luke with a woman in his arms. Lacey never had been able to identify her expression, but it wasn't that of a disapproving mother. 'And she never mentions Luke her son—the other night when she did, she got a headache. Don, how ill is she?'

Don frowned, looked over at the big house, up at the iron lace border that ran around the verandah.

'Lacey, she's never been quite the same since the accident. The guilt nearly destroyed her for a time but we thought she was okay. Since coming here she gets confused, but I'm sure she wouldn't—oh, hell!' He bowed his head and muttered something about getting Luke to speak to the doctor.

Lacey saw Mrs Stewart come towards them with Luke. The woman was laughing. Luke walked beside her, his head angled to smile at her. 'You make me feel the way I used to——' he'd told her that night and she'd known then that anything Luke asked of her was right, everything he'd said was true. But his mother had shown her otherwise, had warned her, told her what he was *really* like and she'd not trusted her own instincts. I should have, she cried inside. I should have. For Paula, for whatever confused, tragic reasons of her own, had been talking about a man who deserved the reputation. The *other* Luke.

Luke and the woman in red drew level. Leonie Stewart took his hand briefly then kissed his cheek. 'Thanks, Luke, you're a doll. Drop in for a game with us if you find the time. John's determined to beat you one of these days.' She hurried off with a wave to Luke and Don and her car whizzed down the drive.

If. If only she could have known that night. Lacey looked over at Luke and held his gaze. She would have spent that night in his arms and maybe by now ... regret was plain on her face, and the hurt of all those unnecessary words. Luke saw it and his eyes narrowed. He looked from her to Don and back again and walked towards them. Don roused himself from his reflections.

'It looks to me as if you two might have something to discuss,' he said in an undertone, but even as he began to move Ruth Harrow came out of the house and called to Luke. He stopped and she caught up with him, slipped her arm through his and smiled.

'No,' Lacey said. 'No, we haven't.'

CHAPTER NINE

'MRS PRENTISS has forsworn pink,' Mike announced. 'I have introduced her to a subtle shade of apricot and she is in love.'

'How did you manage that?' Lacey asked.

'I said—subtly of course—that it cast a youthful glow—never suggesting for one moment that Mrs Prentiss needed such a thing, but she thought it over and found the idea irresistible.'

'Clever,' Lacey smiled and sorted through a shipment of lamps and ornaments ordered for a display home.

'I just hope she remembers to change the colour of her hair rinse,' Mike gave a grimace. 'Or there'll be an almighty clash.'

'You'll find a way to tell her, Mike.'

'Oh no. She was your client and now that I have converted her from pink, she's all yours again.'

Lacey shrugged. 'Okay.'

'What—no fight?'

'No fight,' she said tiredly. She could feel Mike's eyes on her as they had often been since she'd come back to the office last week. Somehow she had managed to give him an update on the Fremont job and offered him a perfectly normal reason for her temporary release from the site, but Mike had probed, sensing that there was more. Though she smiled and worked and talked she was aware that the effort it cost her must be showing.

'You're wearing new glasses,' he exclaimed as she got up and went to her desk. 'I thought there was something different about you—apart from that stricken look.'

She ignored the last bit and answered lightly, 'Tch, tch, how unobservant, Mike—and you so highly trained to notice detail. I've been wearing these since—for days now. And they're not new. Just my spares.'

'Did the others meet with an accident?' he asked curiously.

Lacey's jaw tensed. 'You could say that. Actually I mislaid them.'

'That's not like you, Lacey——' Mike's grey eyes were shrewd and concerned but he turned away when his telephone rang. He might be surprised to know all the other things she had done that were not like her, she thought, recalling the day when she'd lost her glasses on the side of the road. And afterwards when Luke had carried her to the car and there in broad daylight made love to her and she had not spared a thought for passing traffic or anything else. On her way back to Sydney she had stopped opposite the willow tree but had found nothing. If her glasses were lying among the tufting weeds and hickory bushes she had been unable to find them. Not that they had been any great priority at the time while her mind and heart were grieving her lost chance. Whether Luke had been close to loving her, or would have grown to do so she had no certainty. But it had been possible before Ruth returned to claim him. By listening to his mother and not to him, she had lost the chance ever to know.

It was the old, old story. While she dillied and dallied, wanting to have guarantees and promises and exclusive rights, his old love had swept back and knocked out all the opposition.

'. . . a sunroom. We were recommended to her by a satisfied client . . . Lacey?'

She looked up at Mike with her lost world in her eyes and he viewed her sombrely. 'Are you sure it was only your glasses you lost, love?'

She went on pretending that the world was as usual; worked a lot, laughed a lot less, ate less still.

'Lacey,' Beth exclaimed when she'd been back a week, 'you're paying for half the food. For heaven's sake eat some of it.'

'I always meant to go on a diet,' she said and Beth raised her brows.

'If you get any thinner, someone will raise a flag on you.'

'Very droll. How's Brett—did you see him the other night?' she enquired to change the subject from her lagging appetite.

Beth flushed. 'Um—no.'

'Well then who's the new heart-throb and don't kid me there isn't one. I can tell—you get a certain look in your eyes.' She grinned at her friend but Beth wasn't forthcoming. 'Aha, he must be special then. You've clammed up, to put it in your own words.'

And Lacey hazarded a guess that he might have curly hair and a beaky, Greco-Australian profile. Not that she said anything to either Beth or Mike. If they had something going for them, *she* would not risk a word on the subject. She had learned at first hand the dangers of intervention. . . .

And that was all very well during the day. Warding off the images and the sense of loss was merely difficult with the daily chores and exigencies pressing in on her. It was at night that she was set adrift, with nothing to demand her attention but the wishes of her heart and the longing of her body. If she knew she would not see him again it might be easier, she often thought. If, again. If.

Her work for Fremont's refurbishing gradually became a symbol for her. Ruth might have his love, but Luke would live in surroundings that *she* would design. It was one way to love him, she supposed wryly—pour it into a search for the perfect furnishings, the ideal colour, the bookshelves that he would touch, covers for the bed upon which he would sleep. At a dealer's one day, she inspected a chair to match the antique desk already on its way to Fremont. Her hand ran along the silk-smooth wood of the arm and she imagined his hand resting on it—unknowing that her touch was there beneath his fingers. Her body bowed suddenly and tears rushed to her eyes.

'Are you okay, Miss Teale?' the dealer's assistant hovered.

'Just something in my eye,' she said.

The second stage of Fremont underwent changes. Small details that had eluded her were filled in with a decisive stroke on her sketches. Problems that she had discussed with Mike now were solved as if she was in touch with some creative force.

'Lacey—this is brilliant,' Mike said when he looked at a new sheaf of drawings. His praise was unstinting but he surveyed her flushed face, the dark shadows under her eyes and the hollows in her cheeks and under the summer fabric that covered her shoulders.

'It must be love,' he said and her eyes flew to his. 'For The Big House that you've fantasised over since you were a kid.'

She wasn't fooled. Mike knew it was Luke but he was no longer possessive and pettily jealous and he let his knowledge remain silent.

'Thanks, Mike.'

'For the compliments? You earned them.' He put a hand on her shoulder and she reached up and touched him briefly.

'Just—thanks.'

The Big House was a-clatter with workers when she drove back to it. But it was oddly empty all the same. Luke was not there—or his mother. Mrs Simmons bustled about, rather bossy in the absence of any of her employers, and showed her around Paula Harrow's suite so that she could begin some designs for it.

'She's gone with Mr Harrow,' was all she said when Lacey asked, but she didn't say which brother.

Paula's rooms were already very pleasant—furnished with old pieces and ornamental touches that gave her a clue as to the woman's preferences. But there were no photographs around that she could see. Lacey took a few measurements, did some rough sketches and frowned. Poor woman to have loved a man who spread his love around carelessly. How had she withstood it? Had she chided him in private. Argued, accused? Paula Harrow's gentle manner seemed to indicate otherwise. And yet—Lacey stared at the woman's dressing table, set fastidiously with small crystal jars and a tray—there had been that flash of possessiveness, hate even when she had seen 'Luke' with a woman in his arms. And she remembered now that vaguely disquieting flash of fire in her eyes the night she had warned her about 'Luke'.

Mrs Simmons pocketed the duster she'd been flicking about the suite.

'Finished, Miss Teale? I have to be getting back downstairs,' she said briskly in her role as head of the house.

'Almost.'

Lacey took a last look around the rooms of the pretty, nervous woman. What would make her give life again to a man who had apparently made her life miserable. Love—hate—guilt?

Guilt. She stopped in front of a cheval glass—a beautiful thing with carved supports. What had Don said? 'The guilt has nearly destroyed her——'

Oh no. No. Her hand went to the mirror and her image and that of an impatient Mrs Simmons swung back with it. Loving a man who found her love insufficient—hating a man who took his pleasures elsewhere. Would she have wished herself dead? Or him?

They went out into the hall.

'That Fiat in the garage—is that Mrs Harrow's car?' she asked slowly, reluctantly.

'No. She doesn't have a car now. Hasn't driven since—for years. The Fiat is Mr Marsden's. He took the Range Rover to Armidale with him.'

'—he's still covering for him in a funny sort of way——' Don had said. And Luke: 'I've worn all the other hats forced on me——' Oh God. She must be wrong. But Paula had been kept out of the public eye during all the publicity of the accident. She declined to present the Harrow Trophy even seven months later. 'Doesn't have a car *now*' ... was it possible that *she* had driven the car that day?

'Is Mrs Harrow with Luke or Gerry?' she demanded and Mrs Simmons looked a trifle put out.

'Well—she's with Luke, Miss Teale——'

The knowledge gnawed at her all day. Don was there, she kept telling herself and Don knew about Paula's confusion of identities even if Luke hadn't guessed by now. It was very likely a temporary aberration and gone now. There would be no more accidents. But as she left the house by the main door and her eyes drifted over the restored timberwork and the new glass panels, she thought of the fire and her fear took form. Then she went outside and saw a Range Rover parked at the side of the house. Heart pounding she walked quickly towards the coach-house and when Don walked out she ran to him.

'Why aren't you at the other ranch? You said you would be staying . . . what are you doing here?'

'Steady on——' Don laughed. 'I only drove back for the night. I'll leave again in the morning.'

'But Don—Luke, his mother——' she collected herself and started again. 'Was it she who drove the car that day, Don—the day Luke's father died? And the fire——?'

Don uttered a sharp, expressive word and his head dropped on to his chest. When he looked up, his face seemed more lined than ever, his eyes sad and weary.

'You've worked it out have you, Lacey? You'd better come in and hear it all. . . .'

'Yes, she was driving the car that day—don't know how the hell you found out, but I suppose someone was bound to sooner or later.' He fixed her with shrewd eyes. 'Oh, I know what's on your mind. She didn't mean it. It *was* an accident.' Don rose from his armchair and paced to the window, back again.

'But you see, Luke—old Luke—had hurt her so much, humiliated her so often that—well I reckon she'd sometimes felt she *could* kill him. Sometime she must have thought to herself "I wish he was dead"' he made a gesture with his hands, an eloquent plea for understanding, 'How many people, even mild ones like Paula, must think that in a black mood? But in Paula's case, she drove the car that killed him. An accident that could have happened with anyone else driving. A freak.'

A weathered, lined hand ran through his hair. 'She felt as guilty as if she'd planned it—can you understand that?'

Lacey nodded.

'I was there. It was their old place, near Campbelltown. Luke and his old man were cycling—it was part of my boy's training and I was back at the court with Gerry. There wasn't much noise but the car's

engine stopped suddenly and I heard this high—
keening——' Don stopped suddenly. 'When Gerry and
I got there, Luke was trying to get his mother away
from his Dad. She kept saying over and over that she
killed him and at first I thought——'

'You thought she had.'

Lacey began to see that there was a great deal more
to Don's loyalty than love for Luke.

'I wouldn't have blamed her if she'd meant it—
another woman could have dealt with Luke Sr. but she,
well she was too sensitive for the kind of life he led her
. . . anyway, she was in no fit state to talk to the police
or the press without convicting herself of manslaughter.
Oh, I know—it probably wouldn't have come to that,
but we couldn't put her through all the baloney. . . .'
Don had wanted to protect her, say *he* had been driving
but Luke had insisted.

'His reputation could stand it, he reckoned. I don't
know if you remember, Lacey, but he was everyone's
blue-eyed boy in those days. The press loved him, the
public loved him, even his opponents liked the kid.' He
gave a short laugh and a shake of his grizzled head.
'What a sport he was. If he lost he'd bound over to the
other guy and slap him on the back and give that
cheeky wave to the crowd—if he won, well mostly he
won. Anyway he took the responsibility. Gerry could
have done it,' Don sounded faintly resentful, 'but Gerry
couldn't afford any scandal where his career was
involved so he let Luke carry the can. Well,' he said
grudgingly, 'he *did* suggest he could do it, but he soon
let Luke talk him out of it. Pity. What a hornets' nest it
stirred up. The press turned on the boy, started hinting
about drugs and drink. Bah! Bloody fools. Funny thing
is how they all glossed over the old man's reputation.'
He gave that mirthless laugh again, 'Why speak ill of
the dead when there was a perfectly good living target,
hey?'

'But there were two bicycles——'

'Yeah, we put Luke's away and said Paula was with
Gerry and me when we heard Luke yell for help. We
kept her out of the way. Shock, we said. It was true.'

The rest she knew, though she didn't tell Don that. He went on to tell her about the funeral and the inquest and Luke's decision to retire. And she tried to superimpose this new hurt over those she'd thought he suffered. It had all been so unfair even supposing he *had* driven the car . . . but add to it the fact that he had not, and the pain was unimaginable. To lose all that he had valued. His reputation, his place on the pedestal of the public, his career.

'Yeah, they all turned away from him. Ruth—well she stuck with him for a few months I'll say that for her, but she bowed out and a few weeks later he found out she'd been seeing his brother. He was best man at their wedding later, though.' Don sighed. 'Like I said, he was as good a loser as he was a winner. But it was hard, that loss. Real hard. It hit him worse later on. Probably more surprising was that Paula went cold on him.'

Lacey's heart felt like a stone inside her and she waited a full minute for Don to go on.

'I'm no psychiatrist, but I reckon she couldn't handle the fact that he'd lost so much on her account. She was eaten up with guilt . . . thin as a rake she went, and lost her smile. She had a lovely smile. I tried to talk to her but she could only think of the man who'd made her life a misery and Gerry, who'd done nothing for her. For almost a year she turned her back on young Luke who'd done everything.'

'And on you,' Lacey said softly. Don swung around and met her eyes.

'Wearing my heart on my sleeve am I?' he said after a moment and she shook her head.

'Quite the reverse. I only just realised why you've stayed around so long.'

'She's one reason. And Luke—I look on him as my boy,' he turned away again and went on gruffly.

'This latest—development of hers seems to have tapered off. I've been at the ranch with them, staying in the house and watching Paula pretty closely. She gets the odd headache but not as many, and she's talking to him again the way she used to before they came here. Even mentioned the other Luke a few times so maybe——' he broke off hopefully.

'She did that at dinner one night when Gerry was talking about Luke's first car——'

Don's eyes brightened. 'Yeah, I was wrong. Having them here was a good idea after all. Seeing the boys together again seems to have helped her get things in perspective. It's a pity they can't get along . . . but the barrier is too strong.'

Ruth. The barrier between the brothers. She was double jeopardy. Not only had she rejected Luke but her transferral of affections to Gerry had alienated his brother. In the same year he had lost his father, brother, girl and, temporarily, his mother. And the newspapers had hammered him, his public had booed— Lacey thought of that photograph she'd sent him and tears sprang to her eyes. I love you, Luke—she'd consoled, not dreaming the depth of his tragedy. It all seemed so foolish—futile. Now she knew there was no-one who could unlock him from that year but himself.

'As for the fire, it was an accident. But for a while there we weren't too certain. Lacey——' he paused and she got up, put a hand on his arm.

'Don, you don't need to say it. No-one will hear this from me. Thank you for telling me, though I don't know why you did.'

'Thought it might make Luke a mite easier to understand.'

'Yes it does,' she admitted. 'But it will hardly matter. Once I'm finished at the house, his moods and tempers won't affect me.'

'Yeah—the weather's been all bad lately.' The shrewd eyes looked into hers and Lacey fancied that Don was saddened by something other than the story he'd told her. 'I suppose I'll have to pick up the pieces again.'

She turned away. Her own diagnosis exactly. Ruth's brief visit with Gerry might have begun recovery for Paula, but for Luke it was a relapse.

'Hear you've moved in with your partner,' Don said

at the car door and Lacey's head jerked.

'Did Luke tell you that?'

'Yeah. Well I would go and ask, wouldn't I?' he drawled. Nearly snapped my head off. I might end up being decorated yet for sticking my neck out once too often.'

All that he had told her raced around in Lacey's head. She hardly noticed the drive to Sydney and let herself into her flat absently. The first thing she did was to get out the old scrapbook that she had kept so rigidly as a Luke Harrow fan. When she had stuck these pictures in, she couldn't have known that she was glueing herself into every one—tying her own fate in with the tragic year that had taken Luke out of reach forever.

So much was explained. His strain when certain subjects came up, his shuttered coldness and the cynic's smile. But she made absent conversation with Beth over dinner and went to her bed later to think of the brief glimpses she'd had of the unspoiled Luke. The smile, dizzying in its charm, his wit, his pure, unadulterated sexiness and the tender, caring touch that had finally made her blood race and her control slip.

All in all, the weekend had gone pretty well to plan, Lacey thought as she let herself in to the offices of Logan and Teale at an unusually early hour on Monday. Work was preferable to any more hours of circular thinking. It was barely eight and she settled down to her desk to clear a backlog of paperwork that had accumulated during her trip to Fremont last week. Hardly the time to expect a visitor to the office, she thought tiredly as she turned at the sound of the front door opening.

She rose and took a step forward and her thoughts began to circle again. Luke stood there, his broad shoulders outlined against the sun-filled window—his eyes the blue of heartbreak. For a moment there was silence. Lacey thought of that night in the ballroom—of his last sarcastic words to her the day after. A car went by and a horn honked. She tried for a nice, normal 'Hello' but no words would come.

'I brought back your glasses,' he said eventually and

slipped them from his pocket, held them out to her. Lacey took them. They were warm with his warmth, the mark of her tears still on them. She put them down on her desk and tried not to think of them and the day she'd lost them. Words rushed off her tongue.

'Thank you Luke. This is an early call. Usually I'm not——' she stopped suddenly, remembering that she was supposed to be living upstairs with Mike '—down here so early. Won't you have a seat? Perhaps you'd like to see the updated designs for the ballroom.' She bustled to the drawing cabinet and pulled out a drawer.

'No. Not now,' he said tersely. 'I—want to see *you*. Personally.'

There was no other way, she thought, crushing down the surge of excitement at the words. His very presence in front of her was personal—the way he looked, every gesture was intensely personal. Damn him! She took in all the details of his appearance, lingering over the powerful lines of his body, the strong shape of his hands and her anger grew. Every new glimpse of him served to etch him clearer on her memory. With an effort she shifted her gaze, jabbed at her glasses with a forefinger and turned over a couple of pages of her file.

Another car went by, reversed and parked noisily. Two people stopped outside on the pavement and their voices carried inside.

'Oh?' she said with professional interest. 'Is there something about the job that you——'

'Lacey.' His voice pulled her up short. It was deep and harsh, the voice of a man who would not be moved until he had had his way. 'I want to talk to you in private.' The well-cut lips twisted and he inclined his head in the direction of the stairs.

'Is your—partner still in bed?'

'That's none of your business, Luke.'

'Can't he stand the pace, Lacey?' he jeered.

'Don't be crude. Mike is special.'

'But still abed while you work?'

'No, as a matter of fact,' she flared and hoped Mike wouldn't come down the stairs to disprove her. 'He's

gone out already on a job. If you haven't any business
to discuss, Luke, I have work to do.' Removing her
glasses, she challenged him to sit down or leave.
Instead, he strode around the desk, took her elbow and
dragged her out of the chair she'd just sat in then took
her with him to the stairs. 'We'll talk up here——' he said
and hauled her close beside him with a steely grip on
her arm. In spite of her resistance she was at the top
step in seconds and hoping that Mike, if he appeared,
would support her claims that she lived here.

If her emotions hadn't been so threatened, Lacey
would have laughed. Mike's beautiful, uncluttered
living room had a familiar top dressing. A beach bag
sprawled near one of the divans, spilling out a towel
and a tiny peacock blue bikini. On a coffee table lay a
Status Quo record. Near the top of the stairs sat a
brown handbag, squat and filled to overflowing with
trivia. There was a giggle from behind a door, followed
by a low, male voice and Lacey dragged against Luke's
grip, anxious to be gone.

He looked at her through narrowed eyes.

'The only thing she didn't bring with her is the
football boot with the plant.' Then they went
downstairs again and Lacey put her glasses on as if they
were her only defence left against him now that her
fiction of Mike as a lover was gone.

'You didn't move in with him,' he said abruptly and
took her shoulders to force her face up to him. Lacey
tried to shrug but it was impossible with his big hands
holding her.

'The way you were behaving it seemed safer to have
a——'

'You damned little liar——' he shook her. 'Don't you
know you've driven me crazy? I came here today to find
out just how serious it was with him, prepared to offer
you a ring it that's what it took to get you——'

Lacey wrenched herself from his grasp, almost
breathless with fury.

'Why, how magnanimous of you, Luke. Offer me a
ring! Do you think that's all you need to do to bring me
running?'

'Lacey, I phrased that badly——'

'You phrased it honestly, Luke. Tell me—was it a nice little *diamond* ring you were thinking of, to make me turn my back on another man?'

Jerkily he put a hand in his pocket and took out a small case. Lacey blazed at him, eyes on his face that was drawn with tension. The she looked down at the case as he held it out and her throat closed over with a dozen emotions. Nestled in velvet was an emerald and diamond ring. Beneath that was a plain band of gold. Her eyes closed for a moment and the wish to reach out and take them, slip them on and just go with him almost pushed her forward.

'You weren't about to take any chances were you, Luke? When you want to win a game you use every psychological advantage you can.' These rings had probably been intended for Ruth. Just as he himself was. And Lacey was tempted to take the leavings and risk it.

'I told you it wasn't a game, Lacey—you want me, I think you love me. Marry me.'

She turned her back on him and the promise of the rings. Yes. Yes. She said the answer silently, grappled with the reasoning part of her mind to say it aloud. But reason won.

'I don't want to marry you, Luke. I want a man who is here and now—not hamstrung by what happened years ago.'

He spun her about, eyes intensely blue and angry, thwarted. 'Hamstrung? Don said you know about it—do you think I can just throw it off like that?' he snapped his fingers.

'It's been ten years, Luke——'

'Ten years?' he roared and there was pain in his voice, 'It's been like thirty——'

'Then do something about it,' she snapped, driving back tears, 'My God, you've got a nerve, Luke. You come here thinking I'm involved with another man and imagine if you dangle the carrot of marriage under my nose that I'd grab at it. Do you think for one moment that I would tie myself for life to a man whose moods change a dozen times a day? A man who is paranoid about the press and the public—alienated from his brother—a dyed-in-the-wool cynic? I'd have to be a masochist to want to live with you——' The look on his face hurt her. If only he'd said he loved her. But he couldn't say the one thing she needed to hear. There were white lines about his mouth, his tanned face had a pallor about it.

'You don't remember any of that when I make love to you, Lacey——' He grabbed her by the waist and held her against him, 'You don't think of anything—I could have had you in broad daylight in the grass that day and you wouldn't have objected and in the ballroom that night——' his expression changed and his hands roved her back in a caress that was an odd mixture of fierceness and apology. 'I was rough with you and I'm sorry, but the fact remains that you were willing and I——'

Face flaming, she tugged free so that he held her by the arms. 'You're talking about sex, Luke. I know you haven't forgotten that in ten years. But you've forgotten almost everything else except the things you should.'

He let her go then and she turned her back on him.

'I won't be a stand-in for someone else, Luke, and I won't be solace for everything else you lost either. It would break me. You have to forgive them all before the ten years *do* turn to thirty. . . .' Say you love me and none of it will matter, she thought, closing her eyes. The sound of the door stopped her. It shuddered to a close in its frame. Luke was gone. The tears wouldn't be held back now and she took off her tear-streaked glasses and put them on the desk.

Next to the others.

November came and went. Lacey went to Fremont several times. Luke was never there. December arrived with an extra bustle in the city streets, an extra density to the trees, the usual rush at Logan and Teale to complete the host of small jobs in time for admiring Christmas guests. Lacey rushed to finish her article for the DIY magazine's January issue. It was a traditional time for winding some things up—a cut-off point for social clubs, a signal for the television soapies to be left cliff-hanging until February. And a time for starting things.

Mike and Beth decided to get married. They had another party at the flat to celebrate their engagement.

'I'm really intrigued you know—to see just where Mike will find a place for that football boot,' Lacey said a few days after they had disposed of the celebration debris. Her lips twitched as she gazed at the unlikely object wreathed in pothos foliage.

'Will you miss me, Lacey?'

Lacey looked around at the littered lounge. A barbecue apron hung over an armchair, a string bag full of library books slumped on the floor, the brown handbag, chock full of Beth's 'necessaries' squatted on the divan. She thought of jogging shoes in the kitchen, a wavering off-key voice from the shower and Beth's breezy cheerfulness at breakfast time.

'Sure I'll miss you,' she said, swallowing a lump in her throat. 'The place will be empty without you.' Then she added on a hiccup of laughter. 'And Mike's is going to be incredibly full.'

A time for starting ... Gerry phoned her at the office, his voice relaxed and almost smug. He and Ruth were buying a house at Vaucluse he said, now that he had taken up a post in Sydney. Paula would be living with them.

'After Christmas, Lacey, we'd like you to do our decorating for us. Ruth just loves what you've done at Fremont.'

Her heart lurched. She wanted no more strings to tie her to the Harrow family. While she tried to frame a reply he went on, sounding more self-satisfied than ever: 'What are you like on nurseries?'

'Nurseries?'

'Of course, there'll be no rush for it. The baby isn't due until August.' He laughed and she could hear the pride in his voice. An odd tingle ran up her back. She pushed at her glasses with her index finger.

'Gerry, congratulations.'

'Ruth and I have left our run rather late I'm afraid,'

he admitted wryly. 'You couldn't have failed to see that we had a few—problems. But everything has worked out for us.'

'That—that's wonderful,' she said in a voice that shook. 'Your mother must be very happy about the baby.'

'Ecstatic more like,' he laughed. 'Luke's damned pleased too. I think he rather likes the idea of being an uncle.'

'Does he?' she said faintly.

Gerry wound up his call. 'I daresay I'll see you at the match.'

'Match?' Her heart began to boom.

'I thought you might have heard. Luke. He'll be playing at the Cranston semi-final. It's only a demonstration match but it will be good to see him play in public again. I never thought he would ... don't know what changed his mind but I'm glad. . . .'

Lacey swallowed. She had a fair idea why he'd changed his mind. It was just too coincidental that Ruth's pregnancy should be followed by a major decision from Luke.

The news broke in the papers the next day. The champion who had quit a champion, was to play again. His old triumphs were re-hashed, his finest strokes and current retirement form speculated upon. '—it is ten years since Harrow retired after the tragic death of his father in a car accident——' Ironic now to see it summed up so harmlessly.

A time for starting . . . 'It would have to be a matter of life or death before I played in public again'. Deep down she knew that this effort to regain the professional part of his life followed his failure to reconcile himself to Ruth being forever beyond reach. A time for starting *and* winding up.

Three tickets for the Cranston semi's arrived in the post at Logan and Teale. They were folded in a sheet of paper on which Luke had simply signed his name. Lacey turned it over and over as if somehow she might divine the message in that single word 'Luke'.

'For the VIP Box? Three tickets?' Mike said when she

showed him. 'That's an odd number to send, surely?'
Luke had meant them for Mike and Beth and herself
and the odd number was a reminder of his knowledge
of her. 'You want me—I think you love me——' he'd
said. Lacey tapped the tickets on the back of one hand.
He knew now she was not involved with Mike and the
very fact that she'd felt the need for that fiction was
revealing. Obviously he did not believe there was any
other man in her life—hence just three tickets. Oh no,
she thought, imagining herself sitting in the VIP seats to
watch Luke break this terrible barrier he had set for
himself so long ago. There would be no way she could
hide her feelings. She might even cry—and his family
would be there, Ruth. Luke might look up at her and
... no.

'You and Beth go and take her brother.' Lacey
handed the tickets to Mike. 'He's mad about tennis
and a Harrow fan into the bargain. I'm busy that night
anyway.'

Mike opened his mouth to comment but forbore. His
brief period of aimless possessiveness had mellowed
into brotherly concern from the night of his thirtieth
birthday party. If he didn't know the details, Mike
knew that she had somehow let herself become involved
with Luke. Not that he ever put it into words. But the
knowledge was there between them, sympathetically
unsaid.

Lacey bought herself a ticket in the cheap seats. At
least there, she thought, she could blubber if she felt the
need, and remain unnoticed. And by the night of the
Cranston semi-finals she was glad to seat herself in the
anonymity of the Entertainment Centre's acres of
packed terraces. She had a side view of the court and
picked out Mike and Beth and her sixteen-year-old
brother in the VIP seats. In front of them sat Ruth and
Gerry. And Paula Harrow. His mother's presence here
tonight was a triumph for Luke, whatever the outcome
on court.

The singles semi-final passed in a blur. Lacey
applauded once or twice obediently with the crowd as
Luke's protégé won his chance at the final and went to

revive himself to contest the doubles match to be played after the demonstration games. But her heart was somewhere else—in a dressing room where Luke was waiting to pick up some of the pieces of his life. She looked around at the crowd. So many young people to whom he was just a name but there were older spectators too, who would recall the golden days and the climactic end to them. She saw Don first, as he ambled courtside during the introduction of the players. He looked around and Lacey sank down in her seat. She might be in the cheaper seats but she was close enough to see Don's bleached-grey brows and the sharp eyes beneath.

Luke's opponent was a veteran. One who'd never aspired to his heights, but one who had been around in competition for these last ten years. A popular, consistent player and one that the crowd liked. And they showed their liking unreservedly. Their cheers faded as Luke entered. The applause was steady, polite but the difference was tangible. Lacey wouldn't have believed that human hands, clapping together, could convey two messages that were so different. This applause was diffident, held back. This applause said 'come on then—prove yourself'. It died away quickly leaving an odd silence behind the announcer's voice. From somewhere came a single 'boo' and heads turned.

Oh, God, she thought. Not again. But it was some tasteless kind of joke and not repeated. Her eyes were glued to Luke's face as he warmed up. Even from here she could see his strain. Tension was clamping his jaw tight, making the cords in his neck stand out beneath the brilliant lights.

'. . . represented Australia in the Davis Cup challenges in . . . .' the announcer was saying, '—twice finalist and once winner of the Wimbledon title . . . Luke Harrow.' Luke glanced quickly around at the restrained applause and after that he didn't look except for one searching inspection of the VIP area. He must have found his family there, for he nodded unsmiling and picked up the balls for some practice serves. Rather bad practice serves, she realised with a sick feeling.

She sat frozen through the first disastrous game. Luke served poorly and his opponent returned well, making Luke look like a novice as return after return whizzed by out of his reach. There were a few bouts of clapping but mostly a deep, waiting silence into which a cough intruded now and then. This was what it must have been like for him before, she thought in mute agony, watching him as he rose after the first break. '—a man who is paranoid about the press and the public' she'd flung at him in her ignorance. How could she have known how awful it was?

He lost the first set 6–2 and the audience's low buzz seemed almost embarrassed at this humbling of a former champion. Well *help* him, she felt like shouting at the shuffling mob of people. Don't just sit there. *Help* him! But the silence was just as ungiving and when Luke lost his first serve in the second set the applause trickled away to nothing. He was down love-3 and looked drawn in the changeover. Lacey was willing him, wishing she could whisper in his ear, tell him something, anything that would let him know he wasn't on his own. It just looked that way. I love you, Luke. She sent him the message she had once before after an ordeal like this. But that time so long ago, she hadn't known what love really was. 'I love you, Luke,' she whispered and the man next to her moved uneasily in his seat.

Before he prepared to receive, Luke lifted his head and looked around slowly, deliberately. Not as if he was looking for someone but rather as if he was viewing a large creature that had wrapped itself around the court. The crowd stirred, people whispered as he turned all the way around and his opponent bounced the ball impatiently.

'Play,' the umpire said.

Then he bent, feet wide apart and Lacey saw the change in him. It was there in the set of his shoulders, the concentration, the powerful, delicate grip of his racquet. The grace of his old style was not there at first. When he broke the other player's serve and won his own it was with sheer determination and sweat. The applause grew more hopeful.

It was four-all, second set before he made it. The rhythm came back, the long strides, slower now but still better than average, the graceful sweep of the muscle-bunched left arm—the total concentration. His opponent, surprised and delighted, raised his game to thrash out every point as if prize-money rested on it and not an appearance fee.

He won the second set but it was in the third and final that the onlookers seemed to realise that they really were seeing a champion. Now they were generous as the balance of power see-sawed back and forth between the players. And tipped at last against Luke. He lost the third set 6–4. And so the match.

Lacey found tears streaming down her cheeks. She clapped until her hands reddened. Luke ran across to the net and shook hands then slapped the winner on the shoulder the way he always had. The sweating winner raised his racquet to the umpire and crowd and lifted Luke's hand up with his own. The applause, ten years late, rose in a roar. Dashing the moisture from her eyes, Lacey stood, threaded her way through the spectators and caught one last glimpse of Luke, his head down as he left the arena with Don. The older man looked up, straight at Lacey it seemed, before he followed his 'boy'.

'How did Harrow go, then?' a uniformed cleaner enquired as she almost ran from the Entertainment Centre.

'He won,' she said.

CHAPTER TEN

SHE leafed through the weekend papers that carried articles and photographs of him. Luke had been welcomed back. She cut out the pictures and pasted them in the old scrapbook. It was the least she could do. Glue in the happy ending. It occurred to her that Luke had made his break but she had not made much progress in ten years.

One week left until Christmas. A time for finishing things, Lacey thought, and in the rain, made what would be her last visit to Fremont. She had bullied and coaxed and soft-talked her contractors into beating their deadline to have everything complete before the year's end. With the new year Luke and The Big House would belong in the past. Uneasily, she thought of Gerry and Ruth. She would have to get Mike to take on their decor job so that she could cut her connections with Luke. Her eyes went to the jacaranda tree as she parked. The rain had stopped and the sun was out in weak apology. Drops of water continued to fall from the tree's summer foliage.

As she got out of her car she saw the white Alfa near the coach-house. Luke was here. She hadn't counted on that. On all her trips to the house since his loveless proposal he had been away at his New England ranch. In uncharacteristic cowardice she stood beside her car, considering retreat. Seeing him make his comeback the other night had been emotional enough. She didn't think she could bear to see him and find that bleakness still in his eyes. For by now he might have realised, as she herself had done, that love couldn't be thrust aside so easily. Even returning to tennis, his great love, and basking in his public welcome back, might not have exorcised Ruth from his heart. Lacey pulled her mouth down. Didn't she know from personal experience how resilient hope was? In the face of crushing blows it persisted. Even Ruth's pregnancy—an unshakeable commitment to Gerry —might not bury that hope for Luke.

The four-wheel drive was parked further along, with a contractor's van and several other cars. Three of the courts appeared to be occupied, which probably meant that both Don and Luke were down there. She walked quickly across the gravel drive to the side entrance.

Luke saw her and there was nothing for it but to walk over to him. The woman with him was Leonie Stewart. The man she'd never seen before.

'Leonie and John Stewart——' Luke made the introductions and she responded professionally. She must have made a reasonable job of it for they didn't stare at her. And that was surprising, for Lacey felt decidedly odd. Luke was smiling. His eyes were blue and candid and confident. He looked like a man who had been handed everything he wanted on a plate.

'Miss Teale,' Leonie Stewart said, 'I know you're going to be swamped with customers when Luke shows his house off, but let me be one of the first to ask you to spare the time to look at ours.'

Lacey smiled and made polite noises. Funny how things worked out. Two more possible jobs as a direct result of this one. And at one time she would have been overjoyed. Now, when she should cut her ties with Luke, referrals to his family and friends was the last thing she needed. She looked at Luke and was confused. He looked so happy, so young. Had the match made so much difference then? She didn't allow herself to ask the other more important question, but hope, resilient as ever, stirred.

'Now that John is going to spend more time at home instead of jetting in and out of airports, we'll need to entertain more and we need a new look for the house,' Leonie went on.

'Do you mean in future I won't have to get tricked out in my dinner jacket and hang around with you at those charity do's you like?' Luke grinned.

'No, old man. *I'll* have to do that from now on,' John gloomed. 'It's the only damned thing I don't like about promotion. But feel free to stand in for me anytime you like.'

'Luke, I thought you *liked* that supper you took me to the Opera House,' Leonie pouted. So there was nothing in it, Lacey thought. That newspaper photograph of this pretty woman with him had been that of friends, not lovers. Her heart jumped a beat. Luke had deliberately led her to believe that Leonie was more than a friend. Just the way she herself had misled him about Mike.

'It was okay,' Luke's eyes wandered to Lacey. 'As for the Opera House, I like the outside better than the inside. And I've discovered I'm a man of simple pleasures.'

The summer rain started up again. Lacey looked out at it. Simple pleasures . . . sitting on the Opera House steps drinking wine from plastic cups . . . holding hands with Luke on a cold, winter's night. . . .

'Just as well,' Leonie laughed. There'll be none but simple pleasures now that you're in training again.'

The question blurted out before Lacey could stop herself. 'Are you going back into competition, Luke?'

He glanced at his friends, back at her. 'I don't know yet. I'm thinking about it. It would mean travelling a lot . . . and it depends on. . . .'

On what? Lacey had a breathless feeling as if she'd run all the way up Fremont's drive, or waltzed around this room again. Luke broke off, but he seemed to be trying to tell her something and she was taking the unsaid words and trying to mould them to her wishes. The conversation moved along and Lacey remained silent. When she could no longer justify staying, she excused herself to speak to the workmen. Luke let her go with an impatient: 'Don't leave without seeing me, Lacey.'

She was there for an hour, heard the fade of the Stewart's voices and their eventual departure.

'Lacey——' Luke said, interrupting her discussion with the fussing workman. He wasn't smiling now, though his eyes were warm. 'I need to talk to you.' It was that 'need' that did it. Her heart went haywire.

Last time he'd said 'want'. I *want* to talk to you. She went to him at once and they walked towards his study. Before they reached it Mrs Simmons ushered in Gerry and Ruth. They looked different. A definite pair this time, all hints of separateness vanished. Ruth pecked her brother-in-law on the cheek and as he smiled at her and shook hands with Gerry, Luke began to look tense again. Lacey watched the tension grow as his brother and Ruth talked about the baby and the heirloom cradle that they had come to fetch from the storeroom. By the time they had reiterated their wishes to have Lacey decorate their new home, and gone upstairs hand in hand, she had conquered her dizzy breathlessness.

'Now——' he said with a certain tightness to his mouth. His hand was curled about her arm, he was looking down at her when someone knocked at the door.

'Yes?' he barked and Don came in. His pleasure at seeing Lacey seemed to set the seal on Luke's annoyance.

'You didn't come up to the house just to tell Lacey she's lost weight, I take it?' he snapped after a few minutes and Don pursed his lips.

'Nope. Bad news I'm afraid. Pete's taken a fall and hurt his leg. Could be a tendon. You'd better come and take a look.'

'Now?'

Don sighed, moved shrewd eyes from Lacey to his 'boy'. 'Well, I've sent for the Doc. and the boy's hoping for a wild card in the Sigman Classic, so I guess we should. . . .'

'Yes, yes. All right. I'll come.'

He hesitated and Mrs Simmons came to the door.

'Will I prepare lunch for Mr and Mrs Harrow?'

Running a hand through his hair Luke let out a breath.

'Yes, I suppose they'll have to stay . . . yes.'

Don walked outside with them and Luke snapped out irritable returns to his reminders of tomorrow's heavy schedule.

'Lacey—can you come down here the day after tomorrow? I've tried to phone you a few times ... there's something I want——' he began frowningly.

'You've got that trophy presentation day after tomorrow and dinner with old Markham,' Don put in and kept a bland face as Luke swore.

'Well—Friday then. About four.' He almost glared at her, hands on hips and that thwarted look about him she remembered from the times when she'd refused to fall in with his wishes. He didn't wait for her answer but strode off to the courts. Don waited just long enough to put his hand out to test for rain. A few drops had begun to fall again.

'Lousy weather, eh? Looks all socked in, but I reckon it'll clear soon.'

Friday was fine. Lacey wished she felt the same. She dragged a little bit of winter with her as she drove to Fremont in the sun. But no one would know, she vowed. No tragic, lovelorn last appearance for her. She'd made a campaign of it again. Worn a green dress this time too, though the colour was the only similarity to the 'green thing' that Luke said had knocked him flat. This was made as only the Italians could, into a shoulder-fastened rectangle that dropped over her figure to look as if it was crafted for her. She wore the antique gold chain she'd worn for that first campaign when she wanted to get her new, famous client to sit up and take notice, but left off the jade ring. Just looking at that in her jewel box reminded her of the emerald and diamond ring and the wedding band that Luke had offered her from want, not love. Her hair, newly styled, she brushed loose and if her face was a bit slimmer it did no harm to her looks save to give her a hint of fragility.

'Well, Luke,' she could say to him, 'it's been a pleasure to work for you——' No. That would be *too* false after all that had passed between them. She turned into Fremont's open gates and drove up the gravel drive that was newly raked, the tooth marks still in it. What if Luke renewed his marriage proposal? A thousand times she had wished herself back in time. Wished she had told him yes and taken the risk that he might never love her. But now she knew she couldn't. She could manage without guarantees, even promises, but she did want exclusive rights. It must be because I'm an only child, she told herself in wry humour as she turned off the engine and looked over at the leafy spread of the jacaranda. I can't bring myself to share something I love.

Don appeared as she slammed her car door. He whistled. 'You look beautiful. Too damned thin like I said the other day, but beautiful'

'Thanks, Don. I think.'

'What did you think of the match?'

'You saw me?'

'Yeah. Knew you'd be there. Bet you shed a tear or two.'

'Why would you suppose that?'

'Shed some myself. Knew you would.' He grinned at her, more knowing than ever and she narrowed her eyes at him. What *was* the matter with Don?

'How's Luke's mother?' The question brought a different softening altogether to Don's weatherbeaten face.

'She's got a ways to go, but getting more like the Paula I used to know. Ruth and Gerry's baby has made all the difference. She's going to live with them, did you know?'

She nodded, touched his arm. 'For the time being. Who knows, she might even end up living in Gosford.'

Don gave a rueful laugh. 'Yeah. Well, I'm a patient man.'

She began to make her way to the house. 'I'll see you before I leave, Don.'

'You reckon?' he chuckled and waved a hand at her. Lacey didn't give much thought to his odd rejoinder. Her mind had already gone ahead.

Luke answered the door himself. He looked her over slowly and smiled. She couldn't take her eyes off him.

'Mrs Simmons is having the day off,' he said and stepped back to let her by. She murmured something that she scarcely heard over the commotion of her own pulse.

'I'm glad to hear that your mother is so much better now, Luke,' she managed to say calmly. 'She's going to live with Gerry, I hear.'

'That's right.' Luke led the way to his study and opened his drinks cabinet. 'Sherry?'

'No—I——'

'Have one. To celebrate the completion of our contract, Lacey.' Her heart wrenched. A time for winding things up . . . it was going to be harder than she thought.

'Why not?' she said lightly. He handed her the glass, poured a brandy for himself.

'Yes, Mum's moving in with Gerry. I should have told you her story sooner. If you remember I said there were things I had to tell you but,' his mouth twisted, 'what with one thing and another, I never got around to it.'

'. . . there are other things I should tell you . . . things I want to know about you. . . .' had been his words that night beneath the winter branches of the jacaranda. Lacey took a sip of sherry and it burned all the way down her throat.

'My mother was always sensitive, too sensitive to handle a man like Dad. He was a great guy in his way, but his weakness with women was like a disease with him. He couldn't help himself and Mum didn't know how to help him. She grew to hate him in the end I think, but she never let it show. Right up until the last week before he died she maintained the pretence of a happy marriage. Then in public, she broke down—spat out some of that accumulated hate and resentment and walked out on him. She didn't leave him outright but she was in mental anguish trying to find the courage to do it when her car hit him. And killed him.'

'Don told me she felt the guilt as if she'd done it deliberately.'

He nodded. 'For a long time afterwards she believed she had. We moved from the farm to the coast and for the last two years she was almost her old self again. Then we moved here. . . .' Luke turned the brandy glass in his palm. 'She was with me one day when we had a minor accident. A few scratches and dents to the car that was all, but it seemed to upset her. Reminded her I suppose, of that other accident. And the house itself seemed to have some effect on her. She was in a constant state of anxiety and forgetfulness. But her doctor didn't anticipate, nor did I, just how serious it would become.'

'Confusing you with your father,' she said levelly, wondering why he was telling her this now. Was it just possible . . .?

'It's not so incredible I suppose,' he shrugged, leaned against the desk with his long legs stretched out close to where Lacey sat. 'Dad and I were together so much—identified with each other in name, looks and because of tennis. And,' he shot a glance at her, 'I've never been exactly backward with women. Mum had this guilt—guilt that she'd been responsible for the death of a man she'd both loved and hated, guilt because I took the blame for the accident at the expense of my career—though I see now that it didn't have to be that way.' He took a swallow of brandy. 'It's a bloody terrible thing, guilt. Corrosive.'

He fell silent, looked at her meditatively. As if he had all the time in the world to look and relished the idea. Lacey took another sip of sherry and waited.

'That night of the match,' he said softly, 'I knew you were there. I couldn't see you but I knew before Don told me.'

Lacey adjusted her glasses.

'You played well.'

'I lost.'

'You won.'

'Not yet.'

Hope surged through her system. She met Luke's eyes and couldn't tear her own away. There was a lazy warmth about him, a quiet confidence that was almost seductive. He was wearing a round-necked cotton sweater that clung to his torso. A square of card in his pocket was outlined against the formidable curves of his chest. He put a hand to it, traced the card's shape with his thumb and Lacey watched the giveaway nervous gesture with another rush of optimism.

'Well come on, let's go to my bedroom,' he said and she choked over the last mouthful of sherry.

'What?' she wheezed.

'That's why I asked you to come down. There was one thing I forgot. I wanted you to have a look at it sooner but going back into the game even for a demo has swamped me with obligations.'

'Oh,' she stood up feeling cooler suddenly. 'What's the problem?' She pushed at her glasses again.

'I'll show you,' he said smoothly and moved her out of the study and along to the stairs with a hand at her elbow.

The carpet was soft, deep underfoot. No shadows here today—at least none of any significance in the daylight. The house was tranquil, comfortable, at ease in its new furbishings. No longer the setting for Gothic imaginings.

'We have the house to ourselves. My mother's not here, Mrs Simmons won't be back until Monday.'

Lacey pulled her arm from his and stopped at the top of the staircase. 'What does that mean?'

'It means, my darling girl, that we are all alone.'

There was that look in his eyes. God, she could hardly stop herself from touching him when he looked like that. So warm and inviting—and loving. He took her hand and tugged her into movement. At the door of his bedroom she stopped, dug in her heels.

'Luke, I think you ought to know that I can't——' He smiled dazzlingly and opened the door. Then he took her hand again, began to back through the door edging her with him.

'Can't what, my love?'

'Don't think that I came here to——' she hung back, swallowed on the words and his eyes blazed at her so that she felt as if she was out in the hot afternoon sun. She was still resisting when he whipped back his arm and pulled her against him.

'You were saying——?' he mumbled against her hair and his lips touched here and there all along the side of her face until his head dropped to the cradle of her shoulder.

'Luke——' she shook off his hold, stepped back. 'Don't think that I'm going to fall into bed with you just because I—I——'

'I do think it,' he grinned, advancing on her. She backed around the base of the big tester bed that had found the space it needed in this master room. 'Marry me, Lacey, love.'

She blinked, bit her lip. If only he'd say those other words. Closing her eyes, she turned away from him. Faced with this second chance she found that principles didn't matter a damn. She *would* share him rather than go without entirely.

'Luke, I know that you don't——' she opened her eyes and the stark black and white of a poster leapt at her. In the green-gold scheme of the room it was shatteringly out of place. It's proportions were all wrong for the space it occupied. It was a screaming offence to her decorator's soul.

It was a blown up photograph of Luke. He was standing beneath the jacaranda holding a sign that said '*I love you Lacey*'.

Tears blurred the picture and its message, a repetition of hers.

'That's what I forgot. I forgot to say I love you, Lacey,' he said behind her and she turned then and went to him, slowly at first and at the last in a rush, to wind her arms about his neck.

'What took you so long?' she whispered and pressed her mouth to his. Luke crushed her close, his hands searching out the slender lines of her back, thrusting into her hair, lowering to spread possessively on her hips.

'Lacey, I've cursed myself for handling it all so badly. I love you and just assumed you would know that was why I was so foul-tempered every time you turned me away . . . and when I came to you that morning, I left out all the words that mattered.'

'Darling Luke,' she murmured against his mouth. 'I did see your mother that night when I came upstairs to wait for you and she convinced me that I was just another girl to you—one of the crowd with the Annette

Cromers and the Leonie Stewarts. I couldn't bear to be that.'

He frowned. 'Well you know now that Leonie is just a friend, but how the hell did you know about Annette?'

'Etruscan red walls and a Blackman original——' she mumbled into his cheek and decided to forget about the round bed. 'You told me a Darling Point friend of yours recommended me and she seemed my only DP client who fitted.'

'Oh God——' he groaned. 'What have I done? Got myself a clever, woman.'

'Not so clever Luke. Not clever enough to know your mother couldn't have been talking about you when she said you were immoral.'

'How could you have known? Even I didn't realise how confused she'd become.'

'I didn't want to believe it. I wanted to trust my instincts. If it hadn't all happened so fast, I probably would have.' Her tears welled again.

'It was the speed of it that threw us both.' He kissed her, edged a finger beneath the frames of her glasses to scoop away the tears. 'Don't cry, Lacey, love.'

'I cried when I came to see you play.'

'I'm not surprised the way I played,' he said dryly.

'You were wonderful.'

'I was sick with fear,' he admitted, raising a hand to trace the shape of her face. 'But it was a case of life or death after all. Or life, anyway. I had to make sure that ten years didn't drift to more. You know when I stood there and they were all silent and waiting to see if I fell flat on my face, I remembered that other time when I gave up and turned my back on it all. And that's when I remembered the loyal fan who sent me her photo with the message on it that made me smile in the middle of all that misery. A loyal fan called Lacey.' He laughed at her flushed face. 'I almost recalled that picture when I saw the twisted, old tree at your parents' place.'

'Do you still have it ——' A pause, then her fingers went to the card in his pocket, her eyes questioningly to his. There was a strange, faraway pleasure in knowing that it had made some small difference to him so long ago.

'I went looking for it after the match...' he took out the tiny black-and-white print. Lacey gave it one look and thrust it back at him in embarrassment. With a chuckle, he stuck it in his sweater pocket and put his arms about her waist from behind as she turned to look at *his* photograph.

'Were you disappointed with the real Luke Harrow?'

'Bitterly,' she informed him. 'The first time you snapped my head off but the second time I started to fall for you all over again.'

'Again?' he pretended surprise. 'Don't tell me you haven't *remained* an ardent fan all these years?'

'Heavens no. When I didn't get a reply to my declaration I turned elsewhere. I left your picture on the wall, but then there was Humphrey Bogart and Sean Connery——'

'Do you mean I shared a wall with Bogart and James Bond?'

'No. I kept you behind my clothes in the wardrobe. For my eyes only.'

His mouth twitched. 'Behind your clothes ... I like that.'

'But don't get any ideas that I hero worship you now, Luke Harrow. When I was fourteen I didn't have a clue. I was rapt in the image and the profile——'

'Profile, eh?' He touched a hand to his nose.

'Don't play dumb. You know perfectly well that you've got a fantastic profile.' She sighed. 'At fourteen I was very susceptible to a good profile.'

'And now——' he whispered as he unfastened the catch of her Italian dress and slipped it from one shoulder. 'What are you susceptible to now, Lacey Teale?'

'Well, it isn't profiles I can tell you. I'm still as daft as ever though. Now I love a man who can smile and snap and snarl all in the space of a few minutes, a man who sweeps me off my feet with fish and chips and takeaway wine——' she leaned back against him, '—a man who holds me as if I'm something special.'

'You are.'

'Even when you were angry, fit to kill, there was something in your touch.'

'Then why the hell didn't you see how it was with me?' he demanded.

'I'm only human. It seemed likely that you had developed it as an art. Some men do, you know. I couldn't be sure if you felt something special for me or if I was being treated to a great line in seduction.'

'As a great line in seduction, it didn't get me far.' He laughed and lifted her off the ground. She kicked off her shoes as he walked to the big bed and put her down to stretch alongside her.

'Luke, I was a fan once, like thousands of others, but that wasn't reality. When I said all those terrible things to you it wasn't because I hankered after "Saint" Luke. It was because I wanted the whole man, not just the moody leftovers. And mostly it was because I thought you still loved Ruth.'

He made an exasperated sound. 'Women!'

'When I was down here on Tuesday you were all smiles and charm until Ruth came on the scene——' she pointed out defensively.

He snorted. 'I was trying to get you alone—didn't you notice? It was the first opportunity I'd had since I'd got my life in some sort of order and the Stewarts had to be there. But when they went, there were *more* bloody visitors, then Don interrupted——'

'And Mrs Simmons,' she giggled, wondering how she hadn't realised the truth that day. It was so obvious now.

'So you see I was foul tempered again because I couldn't have what I wanted. You my love. Never Ruth. Did Don tell you that we were going together at one time?'

She nodded.

'You'll have to make allowances for a bit of prejudice on Don's part. I was fond of Ruth but it would never have developed further than that. It was all a matter of timing. She had become interested in Gerry and in another month she and I would have split up. She could have begun seeing him and I wouldn't have cared one way or another. But the accident changed all that. Because of that Ruth felt she couldn't just drop me when so much else was going wrong. She was—is— a genuinely nice woman. When finally my bitterness was too much for her, she began going out with Gerry. But because it seemed only my hang-ups that had alienated her, Gerry was never too sure that she didn't still carry a torch for me . . .' he shrugged.

'Timing. I was an arrogant young devil. Everything had gone my way since Dad put that racquet in my hand as a kid and I just didn't know how to deal with rejection. When the papers started criticising and the fans went cold on me, it was a reversal of everything I'd ever experienced. Then Ruth called it quits and to cap it off turned to Gerry—well, I behaved like the spoiled boy I was and up until a couple of months ago Don thought my feelings were more involved than they were. He'd always thought Gerry and Ruth had treated me badly but it was the other way around. Unintentionally my behaviour made them feel guilty. Thank God I got an opportunity to put it right.'

It was no wonder they had looked so tense on the stairs that day.

'I saw you and Ruth gazing into each others' eyes once, only hours after you'd chased me on the road and made love to me and I assumed you were involved.'

'Your jealous mind, love. Any gazing at Ruth was entirely unromantic. I don't even remember it. But I do remember chasing you . . . mmm. What a little tigress you were.'

'Tigress! I was not.'

'You were.'

'I wasn——' His mouth and hands began a slow, teasing exploration, their touch feather light, moving on as she craved more, until she pulled him urgently to her. His body shook with laughter. 'Tigress,' he whispered and she pushed him away in exasperation.

'Just be careful, Luke Harrow. Two can play at that game.'

'Promise?'

'You're impossible.'

'You deserve an impossible man. You've driven me to distraction, let me think you were involved with Logan, run hot and cold. When I kissed you in my hotel room that time you were solid ice."

'Well—I did call on a bit of help to stop myself succumbing. I thought about kitchen sinks.'

'What? Was that all it took to stop my technique succeeding?'

She giggled. 'Before you'd finished I had to bring out the big guns.'

'Oh!'

'Garbage disposal units.'

His shoulders shook under her hands, then he bent smiling and kissed her—slow and deep. 'What are you thinking about?' he asked softly.

'Not kitchen sinks,' she croaked and he laughed again. Her fingers touched his face, smoothing out the lines that had moved her so. Already they seemed less marked. 'Luke, I never shared anything but a few goodnight kisses and the financial statements with Mike.'

'Good. I could have knocked him down when he came here with you and kept putting his arm around you. And Gerry——' he looked sheepish. 'When I saw you dancing around the ballroom, telling him things that you'd told me, I was murderous.'

'What things?'

'You told him about burning down the chicken coop when you were——'

She went into peals of laughter. 'Oh, Luke. The *chicken* coop!'

He looked injured. 'Well, I thought that was just between us. One of those lovers' confidences, you know. It seemed to lose value when you told someone else. . . .'

'I promise,' she said solemnly, 'from now on to keep the story of the chicken coop between the two of us. And the kids.'

'Kids?' He looked startled. 'Do you want children too? I never thought to ask you.'

'We never did get that far, did we? Of course I want them.'

'So do I.' He sobered. 'Lacey, if I decided to get back into tennis——'

'You *have* to get back into it, don't you, Luke?'

'I could give myself maybe a couple of years before I joined the veterans.'

'Luke—why did you leave it so long?'

'I never meant to. Although I announced my retirement it was more out of depression and pique than anything. I always thought I'd go back but—a year went by and another and I lost confidence.'

'But you were successful in other fields—coaching, business. How could you lose confidence?'

'It's the old saying about getting back on a horse when you've been thrown. When I was a kid the crowds used to almost petrify me. It took me until I was eighteen to be able to face a match without shaking.' He shrugged. 'Leaving the game for so long with memories of an unfriendly crowd, built the old fear up in my mind. Of course, I tried to pretend it was anything but sheer funk that stopped me trying again.'

'Hence all the hostility to the press?'

He nodded.

'Well,' Lacey said, 'I'll have to find my passport. Where's your first match?'

'What—you'd travel with me?'

'Lord, yes. I want to be in on all that bowing in Tokyo and——' she eyed him, '—the kissing in France.'

'Relax, darling,' he said kindly, 'I won't make you wait until France.' He dodged her fist. 'But what about your career?'

'Oh, I'm not giving that up. Perhaps I'll adjust it a little. Write my magazine pieces, take on a few choice commissions. Your brother's, for instance.'

'You're quite a woman, Lacey,' he said in perfect seriousness. 'When you came along I felt like a boy again—rushed in like one too.' He shook his head. 'As gauche as a teenager I was, and you thought it might have been a great line in seduction! When everything

went wrong I didn't know what to do. It brought out
the worst in me.' He groaned. 'I've been such a—a——'

'Pig?' she supplied. 'Rotter? Swine——'

'Okay, okay but you have to take some of the blame.
All I wanted to do was to keep you here where I could
change your mind about me, and you thwarted me at
every turn. That rubbish about sueing you, and
demanding your co-operation for the contract. I never
knew I could be such a——'

'Louse? Bounder? Cad——'

His hand curved about her throat. 'I suppose this is
all I can expect from a girl whose mother nearly
knocked me flat with a garden spade.'

'She was mortified when she knew she'd nearly
flattened Luke Harrow himself.'

'She was even more mortified when she found out
she'd nearly flattened her future son-in-law.'

Lacey tried to sit up and he pushed her back, edged
his body over hers. 'Have you seen my mother?' she
squeaked.

'And your father. Yesterday. Re-hashed some eleven-
year-old Wimbledon, had a few beers, saw some
gigantic Bonsai. . . .'

'What did you do that for?'

'Oh—I just felt like talking about Wimbledon, having
a few beers and looking at some——'

'Luke!'

He grinned and his hands moved lovingly on her.

'Luke, I'm twenty-five. Surely you didn't go to ask
permission?'

With one arm he gathered her up and peeled the
green dress from her.

'I'm old fashioned,' he told her and held up the dress
to look at it wickedly. 'Up to a point.' He tossed it on
the floor. 'But I did mention that I intended to ask you
to marry me.'

'Really. Did you tell them I'd refused once?'

'Yes. They seemed to feel you hardly deserved a
second chance.'

'Traitors,' she said, and the lump in her throat grew as
she looked into his smiling eyes. He said nothing—

nothing in words at any rate, but the declaration was there in the candid eyes of the man who'd regained something of the boy at last.

'Well?' she demanded.

'Well what?'

'Aren't you going to ask me?'

'Mmmm. I'm nervous,' he mumbled into her ear. 'This will be the third time. You might reject me again.'

'I couldn't be that stupid,' she said with a catch in her voice and he raised his head to look at her. And though he was suddenly serious and the smile was gone, the loving was there.

'Marry me, Lacey?'

She sighed, put her arms close about his neck and pulled him to her. 'I've got it right this time, Luke, darling. Yes. Yes.'

His clothes joined hers on the floor and the photograph slipped from his sweater pocket to flutter down. He drew the bed curtains so that they were closed inside on the deep softness of the bed. A car started somewhere out the back and as it passed the house, sounded its horn in a four-note blast. Three short, one long. For victory.

'Don,' he grinned.

'How did he know?'

'Who do you think took the photograph?'

She laughed, remembering Don's laconic 'Do you reckon' when she'd said she would see him before she left.

'He must think you're crazy.'

'I am.' He plucked her glasses from her nose.

'I need those for close work,' she murmured provocatively.

'No, Lacey love—you don't.'

And the glasses were thrust through the curtain and fell on the floor next to a black-and-white photograph bearing the legend '*I Love you Luke*.'

'I love you, Luke,' said Lacey.

ANNE MATHER

Anne Mather, one of Harlequin's leading romance authors, has published more than 100 million copies worldwide, including **Wild Concerto**, a *New York Times* best-seller.

Catherine Loring was an innocent in a South American country beset by civil war. Doctor Armand Alvares was arrogant yet compassionate. They could not ignore the flame of love igniting within them... whatever the cost.

HIDDEN IN THE FLAME

Share the joys and sorrows of real-life love with
Harlequin American Romance!™

GET THIS BOOK FREE as your introduction to Harlequin American Romance — an exciting series of romance novels written especially for the American woman of today.

Mail to:
Harlequin Reader Service

In the U.S.
2504 West Southern Ave.
Tempe, AZ 85282

In Canada
P.O. Box 2800, Postal Station A
5170 Yonge St., Willowdale, Ont. M2N 6J3

YES! I want to be one of the first to discover **Harlequin American Romance.** Send me FREE and without obligation *Twice in a Lifetime.* If you do not hear from me after I have examined my FREE book, please send me the 4 new **Harlequin American Romances** each month as soon as they come off the presses. I understand that I will be billed only $2.25 for each book (total $9.00). There are no shipping or handling charges. There is no minimum number of books that I have to purchase. In fact, I may cancel this arrangement at any time. *Twice in a Lifetime* is mine to keep as a FREE gift, even if I do not buy any additional books.   154 BPA BPGE

Name _____ (please print)

Address _____ Apt. no. _____

City _____ State/Prov. _____ Zip/Postal Code _____

Signature (If under 18, parent or guardian must sign.)

This offer is limited to one order per household and not valid to current Harlequin American Romance subscribers. We reserve the right to exercise discretion in granting membership. If price changes are necessary, you will be notified.

AMR-SUB-1R

ᴥHarlequinᴥ

The Winds of Winter
Sandra Field

Tender, captivating stories that sweep to faraway places and delight with the magic of love.

VIOLET WINSPEAR
time of the temptress

Exciting romance novels for the woman of today—a rare blend of passion and dramatic realism.

Sensual and romantic stories about choices, dilemmas, resolutions, and above all, the fulfillment of love.

First Impressions
MARIS SOULE

GEN-A-2

*Harlequin
is romance...*

INDULGE IN THE PLEASURE OF SUPERB ROMANCE READING BY CHOOSING THE MOST POPULAR LOVE STORIES IN THE WORLD

Longer, more absorbing love stories for the connoisseur of romantic fiction.

An innovative series blending contemporary romance with fast-paced adventure.

Contemporary romances—uniquely North American in flavor and appeal.

and you can never have too much romance.

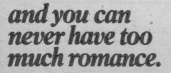